D0499063

Vengeance Due

Lauren Dane

Ellora's Cave
Romantica Publishing

What the critics are saying...

ജ

Recommended read "Whew! *Vengeance Due* is one of the most enchanting stories I have ever read. This book rightfully deserves a recommended read." ~ *Joyfully Reviewed*

"The Charvez family is back in a bewitching new erotic romance. The third in Dane's **Witches Knot** series, it can stand alone but will whet readers' appetites for more. While the story has magical elements, the real magic is between the characters. […] This is an emotionally charged story that really comes alive." ~ *Romantic Times Book Reviews*

"All of Ms. Dane's books are unique and powerful and this one is no exception." ~ *Joyfully Reviewed*

An Ellora's Cave Romantica Publication

www.ellorascave.com

Vengeance Due

ISBN 9781419956881
ALL RIGHTS RESERVED.
Vengeance Due Copyright © 2006 Lauren Dane
Edited by Ann Leveille.
Cover art by Syneca & Willo.

This book printed in the U.S.A. by Jasmine-Jade Enterprises, LLC.

Electronic book Publication August 2006
Trade paperback Publication September 2007

With the exception of quotes used in reviews, this book may not be reproduced or used in whole or in part by any means existing without written permission from the publisher, Ellora's Cave Publishing, Inc.® 1056 Home Avenue, Akron OH 44310-3502.

This book is a work of fiction and any resemblance to persons, living or dead, or places, events or locales is purely coincidental. The characters are productions of the authors' imagination and used fictitiously.

Also by Lauren Dane

ഩ

Ascension
Enforcer
Reluctant
Sudden Desire
Sword and Crown
Tri Mates
Witches Knot 1: Triad
Witches Knot 2: A Touch of Fae
Witches Knot 3: Vengeance Due
Witches Knot 4: Thrice United

About the Author

ꟹ

Lauren Dane been writing stories since she was able to use a pencil, and before that she used to tell them to people. Of course, she still talks nonstop, but now she decided to try and make a go of being a writer. And so here she is. She still loves to write, and through wonderful fate and good fortune, she's able to share what she writes with others now. It's a wonderful life!

The basics: She's a mom, a partner, a best friend and a daughter. Living in the rainy but beautiful Pacific Northwest, she spends her late evenings writing like a fiend when she finally wrestles all of her kids to bed.

Lauren welcomes comments from readers. You can find her website and email address on her author bio page at www.ellorascave.com.

Tell Us What You Think

We appreciate hearing reader opinions about our books. You can email us at Comments@EllorasCave.com.

VENGEANCE DUE

Witches Knot

ཏ

Dedication

ℌ

First and foremost, I dedicate this book to the amazing citizens of New Orleans. Your beautiful city has given me so much inspiration and your strength and tireless energy in rebuilding her and your lives has been an amazing thing to see.

The usual cast of characters has been in play here – Ray, thank you for being so tirelessly supportive of me and this amazing dream of mine. I love you.

My beta readers who make every book better – thank you!

And Ann, my most wonderful editor – thank you so very much for all the hard work you to do help me take a bunch of words on the page and transform them into something coherent.

Trademarks Acknowledgement

ꩺ

The author acknowledges the trademarked status and trademark owners of the following wordmarks mentioned in this work of fiction:

Bentley: Bentley Motors Limited

Cosmopolitan/Cosmo: Hearst Communications, Inc.

Glock: Glock, Inc.

Jimmy Choo: J CHOO (JERSEY) Limited Corporation

Kool Aid: Perkins Products Company

Laphroaig: Allied Domecq Spirits & Wine Limited Corporation

Prologue

ꟃ

Lee Charvez sat straight up with a scream on her lips.

"Lee!" Alex sat up from a dead sleep, landing on the floor, ready to defend her.

Aidan came rushing in at preternatural speed, incisors out, bloodlust gleaming in his eyes. "What is it?" he asked, alarmed.

Lee was shaking so hard she could barely speak. The dream wouldn't let go. She tried to wake up, tried to shake free of it. Running her hands up her arms, she expected to find blood caked there.

Aidan grabbed her upper arms and put his face close to hers. "Lee, wake up. Darlin', wake up! It's a dream. We're here. You're safe."

Her eyes slowly lost their panicked terror and gained focus on him. Her muscles relaxed and she took in a huge gulp of air.

"Blood," she managed to say through chattering teeth.

Aidan brought his wrist to his mouth and sliced it open and held it out to her. She recoiled with a cry of dismay, the scent making her gag.

"Baby? What is it?" Alex said calmly, quietly. Shoving his own fear as deep as he could, he reached out slowly. She was cowering against the headboard. He'd never seen her like this. Even while facing a demon he'd never seen her so scared.

Aidan's hurt feelings at Lee's flinching away from him tore at Alex. But he shoved that aside and put his concern for Lee's panicked state ahead of that. He reached back, squeezed

Aidan's hand quickly and turned all his attention back to his wife.

"I'm going to touch you, okay?" He brushed against her leg with his fingertips. "Lee, honey, focus on me, okay? It's all right. I'm here. Aidan is here. We're in our house. Nothing can hurt you. Wake up, baby, it was just a dream."

She blinked several times and grabbed his hand, pulling it to her cheek and he moved then, embracing her and murmuring against her hair.

Aidan hung back. Not entirely sure why she'd been so panicked by his blood—god knows they'd exchanged blood during sex many times before. But not wanting to make it worse, he watched Alex comfort her, trying to ignore the ache he felt at being excluded.

After several minutes, Lee kissed Alex's lips softly and pushed him back. "I'm okay. It was a dream. It was awful. There was so much blood. My god, it was everywhere. So much it coated every inch of my skin. It was in my throat and nose. The stench. It was death blood. Torture blood. Pain. So much pain and suffering. I couldn't stop it, I couldn't help and I felt so ashamed."

Aidan sat on the edge of the bed and she leaned in and touched his hair. He moved his head into her hand, feeling calmed by the reassertion of their connection.

"Aidan, it was vampires who did it. He saw it, they left him for dead."

Aidan's gaze, which was on hers, slid away for a moment. "Darlin', who are you talking about? Who was left for dead?"

"It was a little boy. Just a little boy." Her voice caught as the memory slid through her.

"Lee, was it happening now? Will it happen? Can we do anything?" Alex asked urgently.

"I think it was a memory." She grabbed Aidan's chin and turned it so he was looking into her eyes. "Aidan, it was vampires. They slaughtered an entire family. They laughed.

They laughed as they tortured and maimed and murdered them. They did it for *fun*."

He sighed deeply and nodded. "Yes. They did. They do. They're Oathbreakers, Lee. The scourge of our kind. They are an embarrassing reality that we do our best to eradicate and failing that, ignore."

Surprise made her face blank for a moment as she tried to process what he'd just said. "What? I thought you said vampires don't take blood from the unwilling." She was on her knees now, facing him, trying to understand.

"We don't. Most of us don't. Lee, you have your rules, we have ours. We live by an oath. *The* Oath. Those of us born to it are raised with it much as you are raised with your values. When vampires are made, they are schooled in the Oath by their Scion.

"But some of them…some of us…are Oathbreakers. The Oath—it's hard to explain but it's more than just words to live by. There's a magical component to it that ties us to our power—to our existence. Oathbreakers repudiate that and then they are forced to gain their existence through death and terror and fear. They feed on it like junkies."

Alex stared at him, agape. "Jesus. Aidan, if the humans knew about this…" He didn't need to finish, they all knew the potential for danger.

"Much as you have Keepers of the Accord in the wizarding world, we have Oath enforcers—Oathkeepers. A kind of police force of hunters. The Oathbreakers run in gangs. It's my guess that the dream you fell into was an attack by them."

"The question is, why?" Alex asked, concern still etched on his face.

"I don't know. But I never dream like that without a reason. Something is happening…will happen…I don't know. But it'll involve us. God, it would be nice to have just a year without drama."

Aidan kissed the top of her head and let himself be comforted by the texture of her curls beneath his lips. It had been seven months since Conchobar had woken from his coma and they'd celebrated his and Em's marriage. They'd hoped the quiet would remain, hoped to have a nice, normal life. He sighed, knowing something big was coming and that it didn't bode well.

Chapter One

ꙭ

Simone Charvez walked hand in hand with her date through the thick night air. The deep-wine-colored dress she'd designed herself draped over only one shoulder and the hem was cut on a bias so as she walked a lovely slice of her thigh showed. The shoes had delicate straps and tied around her ankle. Her lipstick and nail polish matched the dress. She was as lovely as the evening smelled.

New Orleans was throbbing with life once again. The tragedy of Katrina brought the residents of the vibrant city to their knees but the city hadn't given up and so they hadn't either.

Music danced on the evening breeze and stars were bright above their heads, even with the light of the city. Magnolia and honeysuckle enveloped her senses—seduced her.

In fact, the heady scents of New Orleans were doing a far better job at seduction than the man at her side. Empath that she was, Simone could feel his calculations at how he'd get her into bed. And it bored her.

She was more than what he thought her to be. More than the voluptuous woman with big golden eyes and deep brunette hair. More than the sexy, smoky voice and the sensual way she walked. Yes, she was beautiful—she knew that—but she was more. Why didn't they see that? It was like they were all hypnotized by her breasts or something.

It wasn't that she thought men were all the same or that they were bad. No, it's just that dating when you were aware of the other person's feelings was a minefield of all sorts of unpleasant surprises. She didn't mind that they wanted to have sex with her. Fine. She wanted to have sex with some of them too. No, it was the calculation. The intense mental planning they did. Some men spent so much time with their intricate plans at bedding her that she wanted to nominate them for the Nobel Prize. Geniuses really, some of them.

Oh, and well, the ones that just sort of muddled through were bad too. It wasn't that she was high maintenance really. Oh, all right, so she was high maintenance! But darn it, if you don't have high standards for the person you want to spend your time naked with then why have standards at all, she'd like to know.

Unlike her cousins Em and Lee, she didn't have dreams of the perfect man. Unfortunately, also unlike them, she didn't have any prospects for a husband much less anyone long-term.

And so okay, she was just fine without a man. She had The Grove with her family, she had a fairly booming side business as a seamstress and she was opening her own shop within the next few weeks. Professionally, she was quite satisfied.

Family-wise, it was good. Although she'd lost her father two years before, she was very close to her mother and brothers and cousins. The Charvez women were a law unto themselves—strong, powerful, close-knit, magical—special. She belonged to them as assuredly as they belonged to her. The unity of her family provided much sanctuary in her life and she was quite aware and thankful for it.

But she wanted to share her life with a mate, a partner. She was fortunate enough to be surrounded by loving relationships and she wanted that for herself. It wasn't that she thought she'd be lost without it, but she wanted to wake up next to someone, to memorize every line in his face, to be thrilled and comforted by his taste, the sound of his voice.

She sighed and her date turned to her with a handsome smile and she weighed just how horny she was.

* * * * *

Blood. The metallic stench of it filled the air. So thick, so much, that it was cloying. He panicked, drowning in it. Filling his mouth, his nose, his throat. The sticky ooze of it coated his skin. It was drying in congealed clumps on his arms. Sticky and beginning to harden, it was as if the blood itself was what held him immobilized.

He lay there, unable to move as he watched. The white flash of sharp teeth in the darkness. The sounds of moaning and screaming dug into his gut. Maniacal laughter. Flesh tearing. Sobbing. Then nothing but the laughter.

So scared. His muscles wouldn't work. He was ashamed because those things were hurting his family and his body wouldn't even let him cry. He wanted to cry. He knew he was going to scream. He felt it in his stomach, trying to get out, getting bigger and bigger. And his fear got worse as he worried that the noise would call their attention to him.

The thing with the gleaming sharp teeth turned and surveyed the room. Its eyes, god, its eyes. Monsters weren't real. His mother had told him that monsters weren't real. Moms weren't supposed to lie. A monster, *that* monster had just ripped his mother's head from her body while it laughed.

The monsters sounded so happy as they walked out of the room, the sounds of their feet sucking through the blood on the carpet wet in his ears. The sob continued to build, pressing, looking for a way to escape his body, gaining power, getting larger and larger until it was like a hurricane buffeted his insides. A storm of rage and fear and agony.

Feeling rushed back and he opened his mouth and it escaped. He screamed—if the sound he made could be given any name at all. Screamed and screamed until he was hoarse. And then he continued as the empty, hoarse sound filled the room where once laughter reigned.

"Kael! Wake up!"

Sanity broke back in, reality reasserted itself and he opened his eyes and looked up into the face of a human. A face nearly as familiar as his own. Regular teeth. No monster. A killing machine most assuredly, but no monster.

He sat up slowly, scrubbing his hands over his face, the metallic taste still on his tongue. His chest, covered in colorful tattooed runes, heaved as he struggled to get past the fear lodged in his throat with the bloody taste. That storm, born that night twenty-four years before, still raged within him.

"The dream again?" Jagger asked as he placed a cool cup of water in Kael's hands.

Kael Gardener drank, concentrating on the here and now. It was over. Had been over for two decades. But the sweat of a six-year-old boy fell from his forehead, ran down his back. The scent of his own terror was as recognizable to him as the stench of blood by now. He gave a short nod to Jagger, a nod that answered the question and thanked him for the water and reassurance before he lay back down.

The rhythmic swaying of the RV as it drove slowly lulled him back to sleep as Jagger watched, lips drawn tight against the words he wanted to use.

* * * * *

Simone looked back over her shoulder but saw nothing. Still, the feeling of dread that had intermittently crouched at the base of her spine pressed at her. What the hell was going on?

Her heels clicked rhythmically on the sidewalk and the music of Bourbon Street washed over her. The heady scent of the city rose from the very earth beneath her feet. The bag she carried from Central Grocery emanated with the scent of the olive spread from the muffalettas she was bringing to The Grove. It was her day to provide lunch and she'd been craving one of the big, hearty sandwiches for the last week.

As she walked, she let the huge rush of sensory information flow into her and as her gift sorted it, she calmed. Summer in New Orleans and everything was sluggish. The open air near the river carried emotions to her senses like a feather brush. The more narrow streets as she moved into the heart of the Quarter brought stronger impressions as the confined space held it all in. She caught things from storefronts and alleys until she emerged on Bourbon and things opened up again. All over, the emotions she picked up were lazy, dazed by the heat. Even the anger, the betrayal and jealousy were thick where in the winter they were sharper. The tourists from the North were on barstools all over the city, holding icy glasses of tea to their foreheads and wondering how any place could feel so hot and humid that it felt like the very air was sitting on your chest.

Despite the fact that she was a Louisianan born and bred, the weather affected her too. The humid air hung against her skin like a wet cloak. The shave ice she'd had after her fitting had helped a little but she'd be glad to see October. She should have taken a taxi but the tourists were giving them a fine business and she just wanted to get back to the shop. Stupid in retrospect.

Really, she wanted to get out of town. Escape the oppressive heat and stay at the beach house for a few days. But she had work to finish up. She could take vacation from the shop but as a clothing designer, she had to go with the work she could contract, and summer was a big time for wedding and party dresses. She had three big orders to finish and they should keep her in Jimmy Choos for the rest of the year. Not to mention that the exposure was really good. Two of the dresses were orders for society women and if people liked them, Simone knew there'd be more. Work enough, she hoped, to keep the shop she'd just created in business.

She wasn't a brilliant painter like Lee or mega-brain like Em but she was a whiz with a needle and thread and she'd been making things for friends and family for years. The previous September, she'd decided to try and pursue her own business and she'd slowly been building up contacts and clients and upgrading her equipment ever since.

Simone had found the storefront when she'd been in the Faubourg Marigny to visit a friend. They'd been walking and chatting, laughing, and suddenly she'd come to a halt and turned. It had been there with a "for sale" sign in the window. She'd called right then and left a message about the place, and when she'd gone the next day to look at it and the large apartment above she'd known it was the place for her. It was close to the colorful life of Frenchmen Street but not directly on it. She felt it was a great location.

Buildings often kept the echo of the emotions of the people who lived there and her building felt right. Yes, some tragedy here and there, but the building was nineteenth century and had generations of happiness too—children born and reared, love made—it embraced her and she'd embraced it in return. They'd be giving her the keys the following afternoon and then she'd get her shop together with a lot of help from friends and family.

She smiled at that—at the knowledge that she would build STyle together with the hands and effort of those she loved and trusted most in the world. She only hoped that it would come to fit her the way The Grove fit her.

Still, the dread, the foreboding she felt was sharp. She frowned as she was pulled from her happy ruminations. The dire nature of what she felt culled it from the other myriad things she picked up on a daily basis. Each time she felt it, it was more defined and that was concerning.

She wished she could talk to her cousin Em about it. As another empath, Em was someone Simone could check her own impressions with, just to get a barometer on the situation.

But Em was still off on her honeymoon with her new husband and all-around hot studly dude, Con, and they were who knows where. It was likely they weren't even on this plane of reality so it wasn't like she could call her and see what she thought.

Distracted as she walked, she gathered up her thick hair with one hand, pulling it into a loose knot and holding it with the clip that she had pulled from the bottom of her bag with the other. She pushed her sunglasses up more securely and was mightily glad she'd chosen the peach-colored skirt with the handkerchief hem and the sleeveless shell to match. There might be magical weirdness afoot but that was no excuse to look raggedy.

Relieved, she took that familiar right off Bourbon Street and saw the green-and-white awning over the door of the Charvez family shop, The Grove, and took comfort in that. Knowing that her family was there and that protection lay just on the other side of the door, she hurried her pace.

The cool of the shop enveloped her like an embrace and the magical music of the chimes that sang as she walked in lifted a weight from her heart. She was *home,* she was safe. The Grove was *sanctuary*.

Simone saw that Lee was in the back of the shop talking with Simone's mother, Lou. Her mother's distress sliced through her senses. She and Em were unable to read Lee but it wasn't hard to see from the pinched look on her face that there was something to be concerned about brewing.

Despite her worries, Lee couldn't help but smile when Simone came into a room looking like a magazine layout. Even better, she came bearing a big bag with the familiar blue *Central Grocery* emblazoned on the front. Worries aside for a split second, her stomach approved with a hearty growl.

"Afternoon, *Maman,*" Simone said as she kissed her mother's cheeks and turned to Lee and did the same. She looked at them both and then her grandmother as she came to join them, bringing out a pitcher of icy sweet tea.

"Simone, *bébé,* have you felt anything odd lately?" *Grand-mère* asked as she began to pour glasses of tea for everyone.

"Dread. A shadow of dread. Foreboding. I was just thinking about how I wished I could check in with Em to see what she thought about it. It's here." She reached around and touched the small of her back. "Started a few days ago, just snippets. Now I feel it more often. It doesn't seem to be connected to any one person or place that I pass by. I was just doing a fitting at an office building in the Central Business District and I felt it there and then as I was coming up from Central Grocery. It's almost like someone is behind me, watching."

"Like you're being watched?" Lee had alarm in her voice.

"You want to tell me what is happening, Lee?" Simone asked, a perfectly shaped eyebrow arched up.

"I had a dream last night," Lee began and told them not only about the nightmare but about the Oathbreakers too.

"Wow. And here I thought they were all safe." Simone shivered. "Well this is something we have to deal with. I mean, rampaging bands of killer vampires? Yikes! That's the stuff nightmares are made of."

Lee raised her brows. "Yeah. Let me tell you, these vampires are not anyone you'd want to meet in a dark alley at night."

A sick bolt of fear rode up Simone's spine for a moment and was gone.

"Lou and I did a reading. It was dark, shadowy. There is something approaching. It feels like a storm," *Grand-mère* said.

"Not here yet?" Lee asked.

"It will be here," *Grand-mère* said with utter certainty in her voice.

"Right now, it feels…" Simone paused as she tried to explain it, "like ripples. What I'm picking up is the forward edge of what's coming. I have to tell you, it's scary. Has *Tante* Marie dreamed?" Simone knew that her aunt was a powerful witch dreamer too. They needed to start adding up the pieces here.

"She and *Papa* have gone to the mountains for a few weeks. I don't want to call her and scare her if we don't have to. She and my dad don't get much time for vacations."

Simone shrugged. She had a feeling it would be necessary to bring her aunt back and sooner rather than later but she, like Lee, didn't want to disturb her peace until it was absolutely necessary.

"Well, there's not a whole lot we can do right now. What's meant to happen will come to pass in its own time." *Grand-mère* shrugged her shoulders, an echo of the shrug Simone had given moments before.

"Just be vigilant. I can't help but think that this is going to focus on us." Simone looked up as the chimes sounded with a customer coming into the shop and moved to assist him.

Lee snorted and said quietly, more to herself than anyone else, "Doesn't seem to be any other way these days."

* * * * *

The big RV pulled into a diner just outside Dallas. They'd been driving for fifteen hours straight and it was time to stop, eat and regroup.

Minx set about getting them several rooms at a nearby hotel. Kael knew that they had to sleep in real beds sometimes. The RV was nice enough, but a bed that didn't move and a shower that lasted longer than three minutes were things you had to have every few weeks or morale would start to sink.

And it was sinking fast. Kael knew it was time to stop a while. He saw how much they all needed a bit of stability, even if only for the rest of the summer and maybe a bit into the fall. So they'd rented a nice-sized house just outside the French Quarter for a few months.

"We should roll into New Orleans in two days if we allow ourselves a bit of a stop here," Jagger said as he put his beer back down on the table. "And we need the rest. Cap will take the RV in tomorrow to get an oil change. Let everyone swim in the pool, maybe pick someone up at the hotel bar for a quick fuck. They need to remember they're more than killing machines, Kael."

Kael looked into his friend's perceptive green eyes and nodded. He could use a bit of fucking himself. It had been months since he'd had sex—with another human being anyway, and his hand could only provide so much. He craved the soft flesh of a woman beneath him, the sweet smell of her hair, the sound of a feminine voice that wasn't shouting orders or that he didn't feel related to.

"I know, Jagger. We need to stop for a while. New Orleans is a way for us to take a break but to keep on task too. We haven't stopped for longer than a week since..." His sentence drifted off as everyone at the table remembered the night in Mexico City when Charity had been taken. They'd found her too late and she'd started the transformation. Those bastard vampires hadn't killed her, they'd toyed with her, torturing her and then transforming her. That was their M.O. Kael's crew had had to kill three of their own because of this in the last five years. Jagger had to stake his woman as she screamed for mercy.

He sighed. "Anyway, we're gonna take some months off this time. No tracking until the fall. Let's just do some recon and enjoy the break."

"I just plan on drinking some hurricanes and eating a lot of good food. I love New Orleans." Cap was the oldest of the crew. At forty, he bore the marks of a man who'd been at war for most of his life. His wife had been killed by vamps when she was pregnant. They'd made him watch and left him alive to bear the grief. He was twenty-three when he staked his first vampire, twenty-five when he'd hooked up with a very green fifteen-year-old Kael. Cap sported a scar that ran from the corner of his eye to the corner of his lips. The vamps had given it to him while they made him watch as they tortured his wife, feeding on his fear and impotent rage. He'd staked fifty vampires in the nearly twenty years he'd been a hunter.

It was a hard life. None of them had roots but those they built with the crew. They'd all lost someone to the vampires and their numbers swelled and dwindled as people died or went their separate ways. Theirs wasn't the only group of hunters, there were three others in the US that Kael knew of and several others across the globe. It was the same story—loss, desolation, pain and an insatiable need for revenge.

He sighed and looked at his oldest friend, Jagger, who'd lost his wife five months before. He'd had grown up in the same foster home that Kael had, taken Kael under his wing. Together they'd soaked up all the knowledge their foster mother, a hunter herself, had given them.

When the DCF workers had come to get him from the hospital, his foster mother had been there. He'd found out later she'd heard on the police band and had known what had happened. She'd called in a favor with a friend and had the six-year-old survivor placed in her care.

That woman had become his lifeline because she gave him an outlet for his grief and rage. She'd reared him, honed him to be a deadly weapon to vampires. There wasn't a lot of love there, but he'd had a roof over his head and food to eat. She'd understood him in a way that he wouldn't have gotten anywhere else, and when he'd turned fifteen he and an eighteen-year-old Jagger had hit the road on their first hunt.

Jagger's family, too, had been slaughtered. He'd wedged himself into a dresser drawer and the cops had found him there three days later in a state of shock and near death. He had been four at the time.

Kael shook his head as he remembered that first nest they'd come upon. Those were not memories he wanted to replay right then. Distractedly, he rubbed the tattoo above his heart, his name, which meant "warrior" in Gaelic, surrounded by the first protective rune he'd gotten inked. That was twenty runes ago. Each death, each vampire he removed from existence, and he'd gone and gotten a new tattoo.

For Kael this break was something he could feel he needed desperately. Each time he went out on a hunt he felt less and less. Less fear, less sympathy, less guilt. All he had was the pain and the rage and the big dead spaces where he knew other things should reside.

Yes. They all needed a rest, needed to be humans, needed to laugh and play and forget the death for a while. They all needed New Orleans for a whole host of reasons, each one necessary to retain their sanity.

Chapter Two

ꙮ

The first day Simone took possession of her new shop, the Charvez witches gathered in the space to bless and consecrate it. To protect it and make it hers. It was more than a matter of taking keys, it was about taking possession in a spiritual and magical way.

Lee drew a protective circle while Simone lit the brazier and tossed in the herbal mix her mother made as a hobby. Lou was a reader but she had a talent for healing herbs as well. The scent wafted through the air and a shaft of sunlight lit the patterns as the smoke trailed through the room.

Grand-mère laid out offerings in the four corners of the room. Some food, some herbs, crystals and a small glass of wine.

Returning to the circle, they all stepped inside. Lee closed it and the protective wall sealed them inside, safe. Their magic was contained and it felt like water at high tide. It swirled around them, their gifts mixing, weaving. Healer, reader, witch dreamer, empath—four Charvez women, three generations—the combination as much magical as the spell that Lee had written.

Simone stood in the circle, holding hands with Lee, her mother and her grandmother. They all spoke the words.

Powers of light, powers of love
Weave this place together with this witch.
Safe harbor be
From above and from below
From the west and south to the north and east

Air, fire, water and earth
Powers spark and unite
Powers protect and sustain.
Powers create harmony
As we will it, so mote it be.

Each word spoken pulled the magic tighter around them, created a stronger bond between Simone and the space. The spell was of the same type that bound Lee to her house and that was placed at The Grove. That it was something that was part of their history only made it stronger.

That circuit of protection and shelter, of love and connection, flowed for a moment in such a tangible way that it moved the material on the skirts the women were wearing and Simone felt it settle on her, around her and in her.

The earth below, the sky above and the walls around embraced Simone and blessed her with their strength and she was thankful.

Before breaking the circle the four women murmured, "Blessed Be."

As the last words were spoken, the room, the entire building, became hers.

The building had been friendly to her before, but not *hers*. With the spell—with the Charvez magic and the spell that cleansed the negative energy and reined in the positive—Simone's essence became bound, in a sense, with the building. It became an extension of her, a place that would shelter and harbor her, a place that she would in turn protect and create her living in.

Lee then went about warding the shop and then the apartment upstairs while Aidan and Alex came with the rest of the male relatives to help clean windows and paint. Once the paint dried they'd help her put up racks and mirrors. A contractor was building two changing rooms at the back.

Instead of a large counter, Simone had found a massive antique desk that would take up a large part of the back of the place. She didn't plan on being there much except for ringing up orders. The shop would be small and cater to a lot of contracted work as well as seasonal pieces. She'd make most of the stock herself, although her mother would help with the piecework. She might bring on help from time to time, but she liked the idea of keeping the business small and in the family.

She had a decent amount of stock built up. Summer dresses, a few party frocks, some matching handbags and some blouses and skirts. She was talking with a friend who owned a shoe store about carrying some of his shoes to go with the specialty outfits. Another friend made jewelry and Simone had arranged to trade stock with her. That friend had a small album of photographs of Simone's clothing in her small shop near Jackson Square and often wore pieces Simone made just for her.

When finished, the walls of the store were a deep wine red. There was a hint of blue in the red and it was decadent. It felt like you could walk into the color, made you want to reach out and run your fingers over it. It bore a high gloss and the cherrywood of the desk would work well together with it. After the paint dried, she'd stencil protective, restive and productive runes strategically near the doors and windows and around the workspace at the back where she had her equipment—all in silver.

Tante Elise had left her some large Oriental rugs with some of the same colors and Simone had sanded, buffed and refinished the floors a few days prior. They had a pretty cherry stain and she'd put the rugs in some kind of pretty configuration after the walls and other construction was done. As it was now, there were protective drop cloths taped down everywhere to protect her hard work and keep the floors free of paint and scuffs.

The family had helped her move into the apartments upstairs three days before. She'd yet to spend the night there—

tonight would be that night. Simone had spent the last several nights running around, finishing fittings, pulling things out of storage and helping at The Grove. Simone's mother had insisted—and she'd gratefully agreed—on staying with her for a few days to make sure Simone ate and rested regularly.

And quite honestly, Simone had to admit to herself that she hadn't wanted to sleep there until Lee had warded the place. The feelings of dread and foreboding had taken hold and she had them far more often.

At the end of the day she looked around affectionately at her family, lying about her apartment eating pizza her oldest brother had brought back from Mama Rosa's and drinking beer or sweet tea. So much love in the room. She grinned at her *grand-mère,* who gave her a saucy wink in return.

Clapping her hands to get their attention, she smiled at all of them. "Thank you, everyone, so very much, for helping me this last week. The moving and the painting, the blessings and the warding, the hanging of curtains and doing of floors—well, I've always known how lucky I was to grow up in this family and you've all proven it once again. I love you."

Lou stood up and hugged her only daughter. When she had met Nikolaus at twenty-two, she'd never imagined that her children could mean so much to her. But Niko came from a large family as well and he loved kids. Because they were in New Orleans instead of back in his native country of Greece, they'd started building a family of their own.

She'd nearly given up on the idea of bringing another generation of Charvez witches into the world when Simone finally came along. And her daughter had been making her proud ever since. An empath, she still lived open to friends and family alike. So many people wrote her beautiful daughter off as a piece of fluff only to turn around and admit they underestimated her. But Simone made use of that, smart woman that she was. A Charvez through and through.

Still holding Simone's hand, Lou raised her glass in a toast. "*Bébé,* you deserve this. You've worked hard and earned it. We are all very proud of you and your daddy would have been over the moon at you having your own place."

Everyone raised their bottles and glasses and toasted her and she sat, grin on her face, surrounded by the people who meant the most to her in the universe. There were small aches, she missed Em and she wanted a man. But those aches could be dealt with.

* * * * *

Anton glided into the main room of the large house, where the rest of the group was waiting. Some of them might not like human gadgets but his laptop and the Internet had given them many valuable tips in the past—today as well.

He stood at nearly seven feet tall, his hair a shade of red that brought to mind cherries or a fine merlot. He had a feral intensity that charmed people, despite his size, despite the aura of danger that emanated from him. It was his greatest weapon and he'd used it for centuries. His eyes were a deep green and they glittered with an edge of madness that people didn't usually catch until it was too late.

They didn't live in graveyards like some of the other Oathbreaker bands. He loathed those poseurs. There was no need to wallow in the dirt like animals. Far from it, Anton's nests were always furnished at the height of luxury. The mansion they inhabited at the moment had twenty rooms and was furnished with the most expensive and lavish items. Only the best linens on the bed. His rooms had high-tech electronics, his closets bulged with designer clothing. The rest of his followers all lived in similar luxury.

After they'd hunted, they took hot showers in the outdoor bathing area near the pool, the water running red then pink and at last clear. Two females attended him at all times. He drove a Bentley and had lived in this grand style since he'd become an Oathbreaker six hundred years before. He most certainly appreciated the modern luxuries life offered. A Bentley was far preferable to a horse-drawn carriage.

Everyone looked up and slightly stiffened as he entered the room, waiting to hear what he'd say.

"All but two of the Charvez witches are in residence in the city," he said as he came and sat on the long chaise, stretching his legs out. One of the females sat at his feet and turned, running her hands up his legs and over the erection in his pants.

"They're real then?" one of the others said excitedly.

Anton narrowed his eyes and his lip curled. "I told you they were real last month when we decided to head up from Mexico. Didn't I?" It wasn't a real question, there was menace in the voice and his eyes were getting that otherworldly glow that made everyone in the room go very still. When Anton Purdue got this way, it was best to hope he didn't notice you.

The offending vampire kept his eyes down and tried not to be too fearful and yet fearful enough. Too much fear and he risked exciting Anton's bloodlust, not enough and he risked offending him into doing something rash, like ripping his head off and taking his spine with it.

The moment slowly passed and Anton's eyes slid away from him and back to the female who was once again rubbing his cock through his pants. Her incisors were out, eyes aglow. He raised an eyebrow, imperiously waiting for her to continue, and watched her pale hand unzip his pants. Greedy eyes locked with his as she pulled his cock out and licked her lips before taking him into her mouth. The sight of those painted red lips wrapped around his cock pleased him mightily.

"We'll head into New Orleans tomorrow night and see what quarry we can beat from the bushes," he said with a hiss of pleasure.

* * * * *

Simone sat up in her bed. A cold sweat broke over her skin and she shivered, wrapping her arms around herself. Something *very* wrong was happening. The evil that touched the edge of her perception so recently had suddenly become so real and so close that she could physically feel it. The touch of it made her nauseated and she had to fight back a gag. She knew it wasn't there physically, the apartment over the shop was safe and warded. But the ominous fingers of what was coming their way gripped her.

Whatever it was, it was nearby. Not in New Orleans just yet, but very close. The sweat on her skin felt clammy and she shivered as she reached over to call her mother.

Before she could pick up the phone, she looked up to find Em and Con shimmering into the room. Once solid, Con rushed into the rest of the apartment while Em came over and embraced her cousin. The two of them connected, creating a circuit of feeling—comforting and seeking comfort all at once. It was a joyous thing to have someone who knew what you went through, who fit you in a way that no one else did. Em and Simone had always been close for that reason, and a whole host of others.

"Oh, I'm so glad to see you! Is everything all right? You two are okay?" Simone asked as Em sat on the bed. Con strolled back into the room and kissed the top of Simone's head and went to stand behind Em, his body tensed and ready for action.

"I felt it all the way in Tir na nOg. It just rolled over me and made me sick. We went to *Grand-mère's* and she told me what's been happening. We came straight here."

"This now?" Simone asked, meaning the wave of evil that had rocked her out of a deep sleep. "Or the last few weeks?"

"Right now, but in retrospect I've been feeling on edge over the last week or so and I suppose that's related." Em lowered her voice, "I thought it was my mother-in-law for a while." Con chuckled and Simone grinned. Em rolled her eyes and Simone knew that she'd get the whole story later on. "Anyway, I just prayed I'd get back here before whatever is going to happen actually did happen."

Simone told them both about what she'd been feeling. The sun was starting to rise and there was no way she'd get back to sleep after that horrible wave of evil, so she invited them to stay for breakfast. Knowing what a good cook she was, they both accepted the invitation right away.

* * * * *

Lee lay on their bed watching Aidan and Alex. Nothing in the world was sexier than the two of them together, Aidan's honeyed head bent over Alex's ebony one, their hands on each other. It made her wet to see the way they rolled their hips, bringing the length of their cocks into sliding contact. Even in the low light she could see a bead of semen on the fat head of Alex's cock.

Her lips curved up as she watched Aidan's lips travel down the muscular column of Alex's neck and across his collarbone. His nipples were hard and Lee and Alex both let out a gasp of pleasure as Aidan's teeth dragged across that sensitive flesh.

Aidan's tightly muscled body moved against Alex's broader, more bulked-up frame. Alex wrapped his hand around Aidan's cock and Aidan jerked forward, thrusting into Alex's fist. Aidan looked down, licking his lips, and Alex quirked up the corner of his mouth in sensual invitation.

"I think you should help me," Aidan murmured, turning to look over his shoulder at her.

No need to ask her twice! She came to her knees and slowly crawled toward them both, slowly and sensuously moving her body, giving them a show like they'd done for her. When she got to them, she slid one hand up Alex's thigh and the other up Aidan's. Each of them had a fist wrapped around the other's cock and she moved up and ran her tongue over Aidan's and then Alex's, smiling inwardly as they both moaned. She kissed a trail up Aidan's stomach as her hand moved to cup Alex's balls.

Lee knelt then, face to face with Aidan. Reaching out, he cupped the back of her neck and pulled her mouth to his. His lips touched hers and the fire of her desire and love for both her mates rushed across her skin, flooding her pussy with moisture. Aidan sipped at her, tasted her like she was a fine wine. She felt treasured and cherished.

She could feel the heat of Alex's body against her side and she mewled in delight when he pinched her nipple. Alex moved his hand to wrap her hair around his fist, pulling her head back so that he could deliver a kiss that devastated her senses and pulled her under the maelstrom of his powerful sexuality.

Aidan's mouth moved to her nipples, abrading each one with the sharp edge of his teeth. Each one of her breathy moans was pulled into Alex's mouth greedily.

Alex broke the kiss and looked into her eyes, her head still tipped back, breasts offered up to Aidan's questing tongue and lips. Alex's leafy green eyes darkened, the pupils huge. "Suck. My. Cock," he ordered in a dark whisper and Lee couldn't stop the whimper that escaped her. His roughness always turned her on, especially because she knew how much he loved her, how much he valued her and their marriage.

She touched Aidan's head, sifting the silky golden hair though her fingers, and he looked up at her with that wicked smile that always made her knees buckle. They turned as one and pushed Alex back onto the mattress.

In tandem, Lee and Aidan kissed and licked a trail down Alex's chest, stopping to give his sensitive nipples some attention. Lee left Aidan at Alex's bellybutton and kissed up the inside of a muscled thigh. Her eyes were locked on Alex's as she did it, watching his face as he received love and pleasure.

Aidan moved down as she moved up until their lips met at Alex's cock. Alex gasped out a ragged moan as she lowered her mouth on him while Aidan moved between his thighs and tongued his balls and licked along the sensitive crease where thigh met groin.

Soon, Lee backed off and watched as Aidan took over, his mouth closing over Alex as he rose and fell, cheeks hollowing as he pulled up.

"Oh god, that feels so fucking good," Alex gasped out, drowning in the sensation of two mouths on his cock, of the difference between how Aidan pleasured him and how Lee did it. Aidan was surer, stronger, he took more into his mouth than Lee could. Lee used her tongue more, kept him wetter. The combination of them both was intoxicating. Lee's auburn curls tickled over the flesh of his lower abdomen and groin and he could smell the essential oil that she wore, frangipani. Beneath that, he could smell her desire rising from her body, smell her pussy as it readied for them.

Lee moved and she and Aidan both swirled their tongues up and down the shaft of Alex's cock, taking care to give extra attention to the ridge of the crown where he was most sensitive.

Suddenly Lee found herself on her back, Alex kneeling between her thighs, pressing his cock deep into the slickness of her cunt. Automatically, her legs wrapped around his waist and she opened to him.

Arcs of electric pleasure shot up her spine at the entrance of his body into hers. She arched her back and watched as Alex and Aidan kissed passionately above her.

Aidan moved down and traded Alex's taste with Lee, kissing her gently and then with more feral intensity as Lee and Alex joined their hands on his cock. They intertwined fingers and took him in that grasp and he lazily thrust into their grip, watching Alex fuck Lee so hard her breasts moved with each thrust.

Alex gave out first, coming with a long hard groan of release, and then Lee's thighs were untangled and spread as both men brought mouth and tongue to her pussy.

When Aidan's teeth dragged across the flesh at her groin, orgasm exploded through her and her back arched as she grabbed the sheets in her fists. Suddenly a waking dream hit and her scream of pleasure became a scream of terror and both men pulled back, thinking it was something they'd done.

Blood! Oh god the blood. Had to get away, had to escape. WHAT was it? She panicked as the thing with the sharp teeth moved toward her. Its eyes were glowing. No, this wasn't real. Couldn't be real. Monsters weren't real…

"LEE! Damn it, Lee, wake up," Alex ordered into her ear as he held her, rocking her.

Her eyes locked with Aidan's and they cleared. "He's coming," was all she said before she passed out.

* * * * *

Despite her concern for her cousin, Simone couldn't help but be amused and touched by the concern Alex and Aidan showed Lee. Simone, Em and Con had shimmered there immediately when they'd felt Alex and Aidan's terror. Lee had her hands full trying to get Aidan to rest. A vampire in full adrenaline-dripping protection mode wasn't easy to manage.

"I'm all right! Damn it, Aidan, you shouldn't be up like this, it's not good for your system. I'm fine. Go to bed. Alex is here, Con is here, Em and Simone are here, my mother and father are on their way at, I'm sure, breakneck speeds." Lee pointed a very tired and pale Aidan in the direction of the bedroom.

"You think I would leave you to the protection of others?" Aidan fumed. The strain was evident in his voice but Simone could feel his fear, his frustration at being unable to protect her when he had to sleep.

"I'm here, Aidan. She's safe in this house. She's safe with all of us here," Alex said calmly, putting a hand on Aidan's arm and squeezing.

"She's never had this strong a reaction to a dream before! We don't know what this is! Simone and Em felt her, they can't feel her normally!" The strain at staying awake in the full daylight was evident in his voice. He was riding the adrenaline and there were lines next to his eyes and his mouth was tight.

Simone walked to Aidan and put her arms around him, hugging him tight. "We felt you and Alex, I think. Your fear for her safety. But we came right here. Shimmered here in moments." And that had been an interesting sight, showing up in their bedroom with the three of them naked, the scent of sex on the air, Lee saying over and over, "He's coming!" as she rocked in Alex's arms.

"Aidan, she's family. We'll protect her while you rest. You can't protect her if you let the adrenaline ride you like this. If this guy is an Oathbreaker, he's even more tied to the daylight than you are. He can't get to her," Con reassured him.

Aidan slumped a bit and Lee held out a hand and he took it. "Go on. Sleep. I'll see you at sunset. I won't even leave the house today."

Aidan kissed her fingertips and nodded, forcing Lee to promise that she wouldn't leave two more times before he finally went to bed.

Lee looked to them all and slumped on the couch. Simone stood up. "Nope. I didn't want to say this in front of Aidan and worry him more but you need rest too. I can see it in your face and I can feel it in Alex as well. Go to sleep. You're safe in this house."

Alex sighed. "We really should talk about what's coming."

"Do you know what's coming, Alex? We don't. We just know it's bad and on the way. Lee has told us the dream several times. Em and I feel it too. But there's nothing to be gained by you staying awake right now. I have a feeling we're going to need rest before this big bad vamp gets here."

"She's right," Em echoed and Con nodded his head.

"We'll stay here while you rest," Con said, sitting down. Several tall glasses of tea appeared on the table.

After they'd gotten Alex and Lee safely to sleep after a cup of the calming tea, Simone looked to Con and Em and sighed. "I have to go to the shop. I'll take the streetcar, it's just down the road. I'll come back at sundown and we can talk about all of this over dinner."

Con's forehead wrinkled with his concern. "Simone, sweetheart, I think it's best if we all stay here."

"Look, I just opened a business, I have to go. I can't just close down. And it's daylight, there's no threat to me. Plus, my shop is warded and uh, newsflash, I'm a witch. It's not like I'm helpless."

Em recognized the look on Simone's face. The set of her lips, hands on her hips, feet apart. It was a battle stance and there was no hope of winning. Simone was very easygoing about most things, but when she set her mind on something it was next to impossible to get her to change it. She had half a mind to let Con try, just for fun, but she took pity on her husband and interjected, "Minnie, you need to be here by sundown."

Simone's rigid features softened at Em's use of her childhood nickname and she gave a wry smile. "I promise. I won't even leave the shop or my apartment until I come here at the end of the day."

"Let me take you now, directly there. Someone will come for you later on, okay? It'll just be seconds and we'll know you're safe." Con stood and held out his hand.

Simone nodded and took it and they were standing in her apartment. Everything was in disarray from when they'd felt Lee earlier and had rushed over. She was still in her pajamas, hair in a ponytail.

She tiptoed up and kissed Con's cheek, thanking him. He insisted on checking the rest of the apartment and the shop before he left and Simone did have to admit that it made her feel safer.

She jumped in the shower and rushed to get ready to open the shop on time.

* * * * *

Kael watched the siren through the windows of her shop. Her long brown hair hung in curls around her shoulders and down her back. She wore a short, flowing dress in shade of red that reminded him of rubies glittering in candlelight. She was sensual and curvy and luscious. He wanted to eat her up with a spoon and had felt that way since the first time he'd seen her a few days prior when they'd rolled into town and moved into the small house they'd rented.

He'd been sitting at the outdoor café just two doors down, drinking a beer. A prickle on the back of his neck made him look up warily. That's when he saw her, stretching to put something on a high shelf. The front windows of her shop had been decorated in a way that she'd been framed by them, like a portrait.

Her legs were long and shapely, her ass was juicy and he'd watched it sway as she walked. Breasts that made him salivate, heavy and in perfect proportion with the rest of her fecund figure. Her smile was downright carnal, sweet with an edge of naughty, with a cant to the right.

He'd wondered what her voice sounded like, what she smelled like, what the hollow just below her ear tasted like.

"Oh for god's sake! Just go over there," Minx said as she plopped down in the chair across from Kael.

"What?" He reluctantly pulled his eyes from his siren and his carnal thoughts about her and looked at his friend, who was wearing a smug grin.

"What?" she mimicked him. "Her! The hottie you've been slobbering over for days. You might be an asshole who kills vampires for a living, but you're pretty cute. And right now you look pretty nonthreatening. Go and talk to her. From what I've seen the folks in New Orleans are pretty nice to visitors. We're gonna be here for a while, why not get yourself a date or two? Maybe even meet her parents, you know, have an actual relationship. There's more to life than truck stop bunnies."

He made a sour face but snuck another look across the street. "I'm not meet the parents material, Minx. I just need to get laid. The *last* thing I need is a relationship."

Minx stifled a smile when he stood up and tossed down some money. "Okay, whatever."

"I'm going to go see what kind of clothes she's got in there. Could be something I need. I haven't bought new clothes in a while," he said as he ran a hand through his hair and tucked his T-shirt into his jeans.

"Ah, gotcha." She refrained from saying that the store appeared to specialize in women's clothing, but not from watching him walk across the street. She loved him like a brother but the man had a stellar ass.

* * * * *

Simone looked up and barely stopped herself from drooling at the man who stood in the doorway of STyle. He was tall, about six feet, and she couldn't help but think it was the perfect height difference for kissing. So much so her lips began to tingle and her mouth positively watered at the thought.

His eyes, god, they were so light blue they reminded her of the clear sunny sky in midwinter. The T-shirt he wore fit snug across his upper body. Not tight but revealing enough to be obvious he was a man who worked with his body. He had broad shoulders and his torso tapered to a narrower waist. His biceps were defined and hard with muscle. Long, lean and powerful legs were encased in faded blue jeans. The physical package was enough to make her heart speed and her breath catch.

His hair was a pale blond and it was rakish. Not really long or even moderately long like Aidan's, but it was tousled. Her fingers flexed for a moment as she thought about running them through it. He had a trimmed beard and mustache but his lips were plump and firm-looking. Which made her think of kissing again, this time wondering what it would feel like. Would the beard tickle or scratch her chin and face? What would it feel like in *other* places?

When he took a step inside the door closed behind him and she felt his pain. Like a cold river beneath the ground, it rushed there. So much. He'd lost so much. She frowned as it washed over her. Her heart ached for anyone carrying around so much hurt.

He met her gaze and her frown melted away as her sympathy turned to something else entirely. The sexual heat rolling off the man was impressive and it resonated with her. Her body responded, nipples hardening, pussy softening, blooming for him. *Okay then, let's roll.*

"Something I can do for you, darlin'?" she asked in a smoky drawl.

Pleased, she watched his pupils widen and his breath catch. He liked her voice. She liked it when he licked those lips, the sight making her tingly and achy all at once.

Then he had to go and ruin it. His raw appraisal of her halted when he moved his gaze from her to the walls. The sexy study became calculating.

"Yeah, what are you doing with runes on your walls?" he asked in a low, hoarse voice. It should have been scratchy but it was like suede. Still, he asked it like a prick.

Her eyebrows shot up and her hands rested on her hips. "You doing a survey?" she shot back in the same terse fashion that he'd asked.

He couldn't hold back a smile. "Sorry, didn't mean to sound short. Just curious. I don't see them often."

She looked at him closer and saw his forearms bore a rune each. "Except when you look in the mirror?"

"Well, so you can see why I'd be curious."

"I'm a witch." She shrugged. "They're protective runes, as you know."

He took a few steps forward. She cocked her head and looked him up and down. He couldn't' help but feel like she was looking *into* him as well as at him. He found himself unable to resist moving to her. He *needed* to be close to her.

When he stopped just a few steps from her, her scent washed over him. She smelled of sultry nights and flowers on the air. He had to stop himself from leaning in and inhaling her. Damn it, he had better self-control than this! He looked into her eyes and felt himself sink. They were golden eyes, the color of the smoky scotch he liked to drink. Somehow they went with the miles of olive-toned skin and the hair that was so shiny he was sure it would feel like silk between his fingers, against the bare skin of his chest. Whoa, where did that thought come from? He couldn't stop himself from laughing at that internal question. He knew where it came from—he'd wanted to be naked with this siren since he'd seen her the first time. But a witch?

"What kind of witch?"

"You sure ask a lot of questions for a man who hasn't bothered to introduce himself yet. Is that how the men up North act?"

Ah, haughty. He liked that. Clearly this woman took no guff. "You're right, of course." He bowed slightly and took her hand, kissing the knuckles and trying to ignore the fact that her scent intoxicated him.

"I'm Kael Gardener. I'm here in New Orleans for a few months on vacation. We're renting that house across the way, just down from the café." He pointed and she looked around him and nodded. She'd noticed that the rental signs had come down and that someone had moved in but hadn't had the time to check any further.

We? If he had a wife she'd be so pissed off. "Well Kael, I'm Simone Charvez. New Orleans born and raised. I just opened up the shop last week. Would you like a glass of lemonade or tea?" She turned as she asked, reaching for the glasses she kept near the insulated containers of refreshments for her customers.

He watched the hem of her dress inch up, exposing her thigh, and a shiver worked up his spine. She looked soft and yet firm. He realized she'd turned back and was waiting for an answer. He cleared his throat. "Uh, lemonade would be great."

She smiled and poured him a glass and handed it his way. Their fingers brushed and they both let out a muted gasp at the electricity of contact.

She cleared her throat and tried to ignore the flush working up her neck. "How long are you and your wife here for? You said a few months? Just for fun?" Yeah, so obvious!

He grinned, she knew he'd realized she was fishing. "No wife. Just my friends and family. We're on the road a lot so we're taking a well-earned rest for a bit. Until the fall."

Relief coursed through her and she smiled. "Ah, well. It's hot here this time of year but you couldn't have picked a better city to rest in. Lots of fun stuff to do. Good people." She moved to lean against the desk. "So, you wanted to know what kind of witch I am. Are you asking if I'm an evil witch making potions in a cast-iron cauldron and have warts in unnameable places?"

Surprised again by her sense of humor, he laughed. "No. I just, I, uh, don't know much about witches or witchcraft. I was wondering why you'd need runes on the walls. I know that several of them," he pointed to the ones around the windows and doors, "are to ward off evil. Not just danger but those who mean to do you harm with dark magic."

"Well, there are less than wholesome things out in the world. My family has come up against them several times. I've seen a demon lord and dark mages try and hurt those I love most. They killed someone dear to me. I guess I don't want to take any chances. I like having my home and place of business protected. The runes make it feel safe in here, don't you think?" She cocked her head at him and smiled and he was dazzled by her yet again. "You want to tell me why you have warding runes tattooed on your arms?"

A cloud came over his face as his features darkened. "I've done battle with those less than wholesome things. Each time I kill one, I get a tattoo."

"You're a killer, Kael?" she asked this softly. She didn't pick up the same energy from him that she'd sensed on Bron MacAillen or on Angra or any of the dark ones that followed them. Still, the miasma of his pain was evident. Pain made you do things that you may not have considered before.

"I'm a hunter. But I don't want to talk about it. I'm here on vacation and I don't hurt humans. You don't have anything to fear from me, Simone."

She narrowed her eyes and took him in, making her mind up. "No, you don't feel that way."

"I don't feel that way?"

"I'm an empath. I'd be able to feel it if you wanted to hurt me."

He stepped back. Simone felt that rejection like a physical slap. Her heart sank. Many men couldn't handle her gift. It hurt to think that this man would be frightened off by what she was.

"You can read my mind?" There was distrust in his voice, maybe even an edge of fear.

"No. I can't. I can't read your thoughts. Just your general emotions and intentions. I try and keep it turned down, it's as distressing to me as it is to others most of the time." The smoke in her voice had cooled and when the chimes at the door sounded their beautiful, magical music she looked up to see some customers come in.

She turned back to him. "It was nice meeting you, Kael. Welcome to the neighborhood." Giving him a soft smile, she walked around him and greeted the women who'd entered the store warmly, effectively dismissing him.

What the hell had just happened? He'd thought they had good chemistry. He finished his lemonade, put the glass back on the tray and walked out, looking back to catch her eye and feeling more dismayed to see disappointment there. He gave a confused wave and took his leave.

He slammed back into the house. Minx looked up at him with surprise. "What happened?"

"I have no idea!" He fell into a chair, putting his feet up on the coffee table. "I thought we had something and then she got all cool and blew me off."

Minx looked at Jagger and raised a brow. "Hmm, can't say that I've ever seen a woman blow you off. They all seem to like the broody bad boy thing you work."

Kael made a face at her. "What the fuck are you talking about?"

"Oh kids, knock it off. What happened exactly?" Jagger said in his deep velvet voice.

"I went in and damn but the woman is fine. I mean extra fine. Gorgeous body, curves in all the right places. Legs that go for miles, ti—uh, breasts that are probably a C-cup, high, nice." He sighed with longing and thought about her until Jagger snapped his fingers to get his attention.

"Oh uh, yeah. So, I walk in and she's got runes painted on the walls. Well wait, first she talks to me, and she has this sexy accent. And her voice is all smoky and smooth, like whiskey, which, by the way, is the color of her eyes. Golden, amber eyes. Jesus, the woman is the most fuckable female I've ever clapped eyes onto!" Pushing up out of the chair, he began to pace. "She was funny too. Dry sense of humor to go with those high heels. Nice combo in a woman."

He filled them in on the conversation and Jagger sat forward, reaching for the laptop. "That name sounds really familiar, Kael. Hang on a second."

As Jagger began to click the keys, looking for information, Minx sighed. "When she told you she was an empath what did you do?"

"What do you mean, what did I do? I told you, I asked her if she could read my mind and she said no."

"Did you bark at her the way you just did with me? Did you make a face? Look disgusted?"

"I do not bark! And I don't make faces."

She sighed again and rolled her eyes. "Listen up, goofball, I'm trying to help you here. When exactly did the situation go from good to bad?"

He stopped pacing then and looked at her. "Oh, shit. Well, I didn't…it caught me by surprise. It's not every day someone tells you they can read your feelings. I'm not good with someone getting into my head."

"My guess is that you hurt her feelings somehow." Minx put her feet up over the arm of the chair and looked at him like he was a simpleton.

He sat back down on the couch with a groan. "Why are you all so complicated?"

"Yeah, *we're* the complicated ones," she said dryly.

"Jesus. Kael, your hottie is one connected witch," Jagger murmured from behind the computer on his lap.

Kael and Minx leaned forward to hear.

"According to this, the Charvez women are all witches. Each one of them has a different gift. These women have been here in New Orleans for centuries, they're charged with protecting the innocents in the area."

"Damn. My siren is a guardian too? What's the deal with these witches? Obviously they're good if they protect the innocent."

"Doesn't have a whole lot here. They appear to have been here, like I said, for centuries. Active in the community. They run a shop in the Quarter. Not a whole lot about their personal lives though. I can look up some more stuff through the local newspapers, this is just what I can find through our channels." Our channels meaning the information the hunters put together about different things of a paranormal nature worldwide.

"Cool. Look it up and tell me what you find. I've never been with a witch before. I wonder if it's any different?"

"Kael, knock it off. Don't be an asshole. You always step up the prick factor when someone starts to get to you. This woman must be something else. You want me to do some recon?" Minx had been with him long enough to know that the bluster was an act. Kael was annoyed by that, but on the other hand it was nice to be with people who knew you so well and loved you anyway.

"I suspect that I owe her an apology. I hate apologies."

Chapter Three

ꕥ

Simone looked up and realized that she was not going to make it back to her shop before the sun went down. She'd had to make a run to a client's office to take a finished dress to her and she'd lost track of time.

She should grab a cab, the streetcar wouldn't come for a while and even then the trip would take a bit. It would be easier to just grab a taxi and go back that way. Oh Em was going to kick her butt for this—that is, if Lee didn't do it first.

She quickened her pace, cursing herself for wearing the cute heels that matched the dress. Gorgeous blood-red stilettos. They were great for the shop and even on the cab ride over to the client's, but the walk was unpleasant.

To make matters worse, she'd pulled her cell phone out to call the house and have someone come and get her. 'Course moments later she dropped the damned thing and the battery had come out, rendering the phone useless. Stupid, stupid gadgets!

As she walked, she kept an eye out for a taxi. She was at the far edge of the Quarter, if she cut through it she'd be around a lot of people and it would be quicker, as well as having more cabs for the tourists.

She'd just head for The Grove and call from there. Watching the sun dip below the horizon, she fought back the edge of panic. She could feel it, feel him. Dread washed over her, and a cold sweat broke over her skin.

Despite the filled streets of the Quarter she felt watched, stalked. It was impossible to work out where it was coming from or even if it was close. There were so many people around that their emotions filled the air.

She nearly fainted with relief when she saw the guy from across the way—Kael, Mr. hot stuff Gardener—approach. But he looked pissed off. Supremely pissed off.

He grabbed her arm when he got to her. "How could you?" he demanded in a low, urgent voice.

She tried to pull her arm back but he held it tight. "Let go of me! What the hell is wrong with you? How could I what?" Great, he was a nutbag! Crazy evil vampires and nutbags—oh, just a normal night in the Crescent City.

"You have one of them in your family? Don't you know he'll kill all of you? They're all a bunch of animals. Are you one of their daytime servants? Someone to fuck while you lure others for him to kill?"

She reared back and slapped him so hard the contact reverberated up her arm. "You let go of me now, you crazy prick!" she hissed. "How dare you talk to me like this? You come into my shop and flirt until you find out I'm an empath. Then you run the other way. What's your glitch anyway? You're back here now, looking for me to accuse me of what exactly?"

Kael put a hand up to his face. She seemed genuinely upset. He couldn't understand it. If she was with the vampires—and the information Jagger found sure pointed to her having one in the damned family—she shouldn't be so upset. In fact, she seemed afraid. She kept looking around, eyes darting, the fear in them clear. But did she actually sound hurt that he'd left her shop? He hadn't run! But even if he had, she was with *them*. He hardened his resolve and pushed her back into the alley behind them.

"Look, I don't know what this is about but we need to stay on the public sidewalk. There's something bad out here tonight," she said urgently.

"Yeah, your cousin's husband!"

"What? Aidan? Alex? Con? What are you talking about? Are you off your medication or something?" She tried to push him out of the alley but he didn't budge. Her nose wrinkled as wetness oozed into her shoe. She looked down and saw the damage and glared back at him. "Damn you, I stepped in a puddle of something! These shoes cost me three hundred dollars!"

"You're talking about shoes? I'm talking about vampires. You're with them!"

She looked at him openmouthed. "What vampires? I'm not *with* any vampires. But damn you, stud boy, we're going to bump into some nasty ones if we don't get the hell out of here and now!" It hit her, the wave of dread and terror, so hard that it caused her to double over and retch.

The anger in his voice turned to concern. The hard hands at her upper arms went gentle. "Are you all right? Are you running from them? I can help you. I'm a hunter. We can get you out of the city and destroy them and their nest."

"Are you listening to me? They're coming!" Panic was choking her, she pounded on his chest to try and get past him. "We have to get out of here!"

"How do you know? Are they following you? We'll get back to the house, come on." He spun to take her back out to the street but his way was blocked.

"Well, it's a hunter," the vampire at the mouth of the alley said in a menacing purr as he sinuously stalked toward them. He was tall and his deep red hair was long and lifted on the humid breeze. His very being emanated menace and yet sex—a wild thing. Dangerous. He sniffed at the breeze and narrowed his eyes at Simone. "And a witch too. Oh this is rich! I'm betting a Charvez. My, my, my." He licked his gleaming, needle-thin, sharp incisors. "Oh you're going to be tasty," he purred.

"I told you," she couldn't resist hissing at Kael, who gave her an annoyed look.

"Well how did you know?" he hissed back.

"God, are you as stupid as you're good-looking? I *told* you, I'm an empath. A feeler. I've felt this energy coming for a few weeks now. I was on my way to a safe place when you ambushed me and went all tough guy on me. Shoved me into this alley. An alley! You must be pretty lucky or you've never seen a vampire before because I have a hard time believing you're still alive if you routinely act so dumb!"

The vampire watched them with extreme fascination.

"Dumb? You're the one related to fucking vampires! How's that for dumb? Did you think that it would never come to bite you on the ass because you were too pretty to ever suffer the consequences?"

She gasped in shock and turned to him, slapping him soundly on the other cheek. "You don't know a thing about me! Too pretty? Ugh! Ego much, asshole?" How could she have been attracted to this Neanderthal? And because of his attitude she was in an alley with some Hannibal Lecter vampire. "This is your fault! Aidan isn't like this vampire. He would never hurt anyone in anything other than self-defense." Out of the corner of her eye she saw the vampire moving, and two more stepped to his right and to his left. Great.

Kael knew there were now three of them and he moved to put himself between the siren and the vampires. He'd left the modified sawed-off at the house like a fool but he remembered the Berettas. One sat under each arm, and he had a knife in his boot. Problem was, he could feel that this one was old. If this vamp was Anton Perdue, he was in big trouble. Perdue was the vampire his hunters had been trailing for the last months.

"As fascinating as this lovers' quarrel is, I'm quite hungry and you've made a lot of trouble for my people, hunter. And this tasty piece is going to recharge my batteries in a big way." He looked around Kael to Simone. "Oh yes, she is. I've not had my way with a witch in a hundred and fifty years. I think I'll play with you a while in front of her, get her nice and terrified." His voice was poisonous, laced with fear and horror.

Kael knew the tricks but still it made him sick in his guts. He fought his muscles when they wanted to tremble.

"Listen to me, when I say run, run," Kael said quietly, head turned slightly.

Simone reached down and slid her shoes off. He could see her nodding her head. "I'll get help," she said quietly, never taking her eyes off the vampires at the mouth of the alley.

"Get down," Kael said. He dimly heard her body hit the pavement as he dropped and rolled to the side, pulling both guns as he did. He pushed everything else out of his head as he concentrated on head shots. The oldest vamp, clearly the leader of the group, was a blur and a bullet hit the side of the building.

He hit one of the other vamps, but not with a head shot. The special silver bullets would slowly kill him if they weren't removed but that wasn't going to be of much help right then.

The third vampire was on him then, hand gripping his throat. His razor-sharp teeth glinted in the yellow light of the streetlamp. That light taunted Kael, the street was so close yet so far away. He could feel the magic from the old one, knew that people would just walk right by the alley without seeing or hearing anything strange.

The vampire held Kael's right wrist in his free hand. Lucky for him, he was an excellent shot with either, and he smiled in grim triumph at the surprised look the vamp wore as he crumpled to the ground and then began to dissolve.

He heard Simone's scream and wrenched around to see what was happening. Enraged, Kael watched the vampire lean in to taste the blood welling on the swelled lip it'd given her. In slow motion, Kael raised his weapons up to shoot the old one in the head. Before he could get a shot off, Kael was sent sprawling across the alley by the other vampire.

"Come on, hunter, not very sporting of you. You with your guns and me with none," the vampire taunted as he moved toward Kael's slumped form. Dimly Kael knew that his left wrist had been broken and the shoulder was dislocated.

Simone screamed again, the terror in the sound shot straight to Kael's heart. In the brief moment that he shifted his attention, the vampire was on him.

* * * * *

Simone could barely breathe through the fear and panic. It was more than her own emotions—she knew she was picking up on the thrall the red-headed vampire was pushing at her. He emanated evil. Dripped with loathing and dread. She'd never felt anything like it before.

She shook off the trancelike state and looked for a way out. The only way was past the vampires at the opening of the alley. Problem was how to get past them. Kael was busy kicking ass so she couldn't count on his help with that. Plus, she couldn't abandon him there. Frantically, she dug through her purse, found the canister of pepper spray there and pulled it out, holding it to her side.

"Well hello, pretty. I don't believe I've introduced myself yet. How remiss of me. As you and I will be quite intimate for the next little while, we should start getting to know each other." His voice was so beautiful, filled with wonderful things. He bowed and held out his hand. "I'm Anton Perdue, it's my pleasure to meet you. You are a Charvez, are you not?"

Simone stood up and walked a step toward him and then the reality of the situation came crashing through his thrall, bringing her to a stunned halt.

"Ah, yes, you are above average aren't you, pretty?" Anton purred.

"I'm not your pretty, bucko."

Anton raised a brow and two things happened simultaneously—his hand whipped out faster than she could see, striking her face so hard her head snapped back with a jolt, and she was overcome with images of death. She grabbed her stomach and bent in two, the canister falling from her fingers. She screamed as she fought, drowning in the misery he broadcast.

She hit the ground, seeing stars as her head cracked against the concrete. Unable to concentrate, she couldn't hold back the rush of emotions from the city around her, from this monster looming over her.

Death, misery, destruction, anger, violence, rage, hopelessness, fear—all of the most base and paralyzing of emotions battered her, overwhelmed her brain. Her gift couldn't process it all and handle her own fear as well. She could feel herself begging to shut down, disconnect.

Anton leaned down and when he touched her, she saw inside him and screamed again. She didn't want to give him her scream, her pain, but she had no way to stop it from hurtling out of her.

He had her by the front of her dress, she heard it rip in his grasp. With a casual movement of his wrist he slammed her back against the ground hard enough that she grunted. Her arm flailed out. She touched the edge of her shoe and grabbed it.

He leaned in to lick the blood that had welled on her lip and she connected with the side of his face, the heel breaking the skin. With a scream of rage he yanked her head back and she felt his teeth tear into the tender flesh of her neck. Searing, terrible pain ripped through her body. She heard the wet sounds of his attack and she screamed out loud and long, sending her terror into the night air in the alley.

Her scream died as she began to lose consciousness. Suddenly his body flew across the alley and hit the wall. Simone's last sight was of Aidan, teeth bared in a feral snarl.

* * * * *

Con shimmered back into the house. Simone's unconscious body was in his arms and she was still bleeding profusely from the wound on her neck. He stalked to the couch and put her down carefully.

"I'll be back," he said shortly and was gone.

Lee rushed to her cousin, joined by Em, who looked at Lee with alarm.

"I can't feel her, Lee. I can't feel a thing from her!"

Before they could utter another word Con shimmered back holding Kael and deposited him on the other couch, and in two more trips had returned with Alex and then Aidan.

"What the hell happened?" Lee demanded as Aidan rushed into the kitchen to get clean cloths and the healing herbs, returning to Simone's side.

"The Oathbreaker bit her," Aidan said tersely, cleansing the wound and then packing it with the herbs.

"Is she going to be all right?" Lee asked anxiously, watching him work.

"I don't know!" He looked up at her and his pain was clear in his face. "It depends on how much blood he took and whether she ingested any of his. I don't know what a bite would be like for an empath. He would have flooded her mind with terror as he bit her, to build up her fear so he could feed off it."

Lee began to pace. Em looked at Con and he gave a slight shrug. She closed her eyes for a moment. "Who's this?" she asked, looking at the tattooed, pierced, unconscious man on her couch.

"He was fighting one of the Oathbreakers. From the looks of the pile of ashes in the alley, he killed at least one of them. He's all right, a broken wrist, some other moderate wounds, perhaps a concussion and," Con passed a hand over Kael's shoulder, "a dislocated shoulder. I've repaired the break and put the shoulder back into the joint."

"What happened? Where did you find them? Who is he?" Lee repeated.

"They were in an alley about four blocks from The Grove. The Oathbreakers had a spell on it, people were just walking by. When Simone broadcast that last bit of her terror and Em felt it, I was able to locate her through Em." Con sighed. "I don't know who the hell the man is but he was fighting a three-hundred-year-old Oathbreaker with a dislocated shoulder and a broken wrist. He's a warrior." The last was said with solemn respect.

"Well, he's in pain. Emotional pain," Em clarified as she looked between Kael and Simone. "A lot of it."

Lee brushed Simone's hair away from her face, took the washcloth from Aidan and did her best to gently clean the blood from her cousin's face and chest. "I hope you killed that Oathbreaker bastard."

Aidan sighed as he sat on the floor at Lee's feet. "No. I'm sorry. When we got there, I threw him off her and Con brought her straight back here. We tangled, the Oathbreaker and me. He's old, Lee. At least twice my age and he's got a lot of magic. He got away."

"All of the death has fueled his magic," Alex said, bringing a clean shirt in for Lee and Em to change Simone into. The men turned their backs as Lee and Em pulled the tatters of Simone's dress from her battered body and gently got her into the shirt.

"You have to use silver on them, nothing else can kill them. And with one as old as Anton Perdue, you'd better shoot him between the eyes."

They all turned to face Kael, who was trying to sit up. Con let him grab his hand and pull himself upright.

"Take it slow. You should be all right, my healing spells are pretty good after ten thousand years, but there's no use taking chances."

Kael looked at him with narrowed eyes. "What are you, then?"

Con raised a brow and chuckled. "I am Conchobar MacNessa, and you are in the home of Lee Charvez, Alex Carter and Aidan Bell. Is there any soreness?"

"Aidan Bell! The vampire? Where is the butcher, then?" Kael pushed himself to his feet, ready to fight although it was clear that he was still shaky.

Aidan stared up at him from his place on the floor in front of Simone. Lee stepped forward but Aidan put his arm out to stop her. "Careful, human. You're in my home and I just saved your life. Add that to the fact that you were in an alley with my wife's cousin, who was being ravaged by an Oathbreaker and *you're* the one on shaky ground."

Em watched Kael as his eyes moved from Aidan to Simone. *Oh, it couldn't be!* She closed her eyes and opened herself up to him, examined his feelings, his motivations. The bright ember of who he was to Simone smoldered deep but it was there nonetheless.

"You can't kill him, Aidan," Em said quietly. "And you, show some manners," she addressed Kael.

"Is she all right? It bit her? Did it change her?" Kael winced as he moved across to the couch Simone was on. Falling to his knees, he leaned in close to her, examining her face hungrily. Em sighed. One didn't have to be an empath to hear the anguish in his voice.

Before anyone could answer, a pounding on the door got their attention and Alex went to investigate. Moments later Lou hurried into the room and to her daughter's side. Marie came in after her and went to Lee's side anxiously.

"*Chérie!* Baby, *Maman* is here. Wake up," she urged with tears in her voice.

Lee quietly explained to her mother and *Tante* Lou what they knew so far and Kael sat back and watched the exchange. He watched Aidan treat who he guessed was his woman with affection and gentleness. He couldn't quite wrap his head around it and he didn't want to.

Coming to his feet quickly, he went to the tall dark-haired woman with the expressive eyes. "What of the vampire in the alley?"

"He got away," Con said, overhearing the question.

"I've got to go find him." He moved toward the door and looked back over his shoulder to his siren, pale and unconscious on the couch. It was better this way. He couldn't trust her, couldn't offer her anything more than a few nights in his bed.

"Wait! Who are you?" Alex asked, careful not to touch the clearly agitated man.

"I'm Kael Gardener. I kill vampires."

Aidan stood up and Con moved where he could aid or intervene as needed. "You're a vampire hunter?"

"Yes. I'm only leaving you alive so you can help Simone. But after tonight, if I see you, I'll kill you." He looked at the rest of the people in the room. "I don't know how he's managed to snow you all—maybe you all know what vampires do." He shrugged, not knowing if they were in on the vampire's misdeeds or not. "But they can't be tamed and sooner or later you'll end up dead. Get out while you can."

"You don't know what you're talking about, son. I get the feeling something bad happened to you and Oathbreakers are responsible. But you don't know the whole story and that makes you dangerous." Con stepped in Kael's path.

"Damned right I'm dangerous. Now, if you'll excuse me. Please, take care of her," he added softly just before he barged out the door and into the night.

"He's alone. The old one is still out there. Con, will you do the idiot a favor and shimmer him back home?" Aidan's voice was weary.

Con nodded and went out to catch up with Kael.

Em sat with her arm around her aunt. "She's going to be all right. I couldn't feel her before but I can now. She's coming back to herself."

Lou looked up at Aidan. "Will she be a vampire now?"

Aidan shook his head. "No. He bit her but it takes more than that. It's complicated, but rest assured that this did not happen with our Simone. I was concerned but she's not manifesting any signs of taking his blood."

"Are you all right?" Lee murmured, taking in Aidan's strained features.

"This is my fault, Lee."

She put her hands up, cradling his face. "This is not your fault, Aidan. No more than Angra was Alex's fault. There are bad people in the world. You didn't make this vampire break his Oath. You didn't make him hurt Minnie. You know she won't blame you. I don't blame you. No one is blaming you but you."

"You don't understand!" He pulled back and began to pace. "My family holds a very powerful position in the vampire nation. I have a duty to my people! My brother Connor is an Oathkeeper. I should have called him immediately when you first dreamed. But I didn't want to deal with this, didn't want to face it. And then this morning I was so terrified for you I forgot, and then we rushed off to get Simone. I have to call him and we've got to get the Keepers here. If they were here already, they could have taken care of Perdue in that alley tonight."

"Call him now and stop blaming yourself. It's over and done, Aidan. There's no good to come of your guilt," Lou said quietly, looking up from where she'd been sitting, holding Simone's hand.

Aidan nodded quickly and headed out of the room.

"Thank you," Lee said, squeezing her aunt's shoulder.

Lou nodded. "No use parsing blame now."

* * * * *

Aidan dialed his brother's cell phone number, relaying the tale as quickly and succinctly as possible. He hung up ten minutes later and went back into the comfortable living room, where more of the family had gathered.

"He's coming now. How is she?"

"She's moving a bit more. Em can feel her again, she's pulling back into herself." Relief was clear in Lee's tone as she handed him a glass of lemonade.

"Should we move her to one of the beds upstairs?"

"No, let's just keep her here for the next hour or so." Aidan's voice held something in it that made Lou look up sharply.

"What is it you aren't saying?"

Aidan sighed. "Sometimes when someone is bitten, a connection can be created between the vampire and the victim. Because Simone is an empath I just want to have her in this room where Lee and Alex routinely practice their magic. As an extra level of protection from any possible outside danger. Just for a few hours."

"Oh it just gets better and better doesn't it?" Lou said sarcastically. "What does this mean for her? Will he be able to control her? Make her do things he wants her to?"

Aidan shook his head. "No. But she'd pick up his emotions like he was in the same room. He might be able to feel what she feels."

"Could he spy on us through her?" Alex asked.

"No, it's not like that. But he may be able to feed off her emotions. We'll have to wait and see."

Several people heaved heavy sighs and settled in to watch over Simone's recovery.

* * * * *

"Kael," Con called out, jogging to catch up with the retreating man.

Kael turned and made an impatient sound as he exhaled. "What?"

"Listen, this Oathbreaker is still out there. Let me at least get you home safely. I assume you have a secure residence here in New Orleans?"

As he had no real idea of where he was or how to get back to the house, he stopped and nodded shortly. "Fine, where's your car?"

Con rolled his eyes. "Again, let me point out that you don't know the whole story, not by a long shot. I'm a Faerie, think of the location you wish to go and we'll be there." Con reached out and touched Kael's arm as he said this.

"Faerie?" But even as Kael asked, he thought of their place back in the Faubourg Marigny and they were standing there, Con wearing a smug look and Jagger on his feet pointing a gun.

"Human, put that down," Con said calmly and Kael nodded shortly, resulting in Jagger lowering the weapon and looking wide-eyed at them both.

"What the hell is going on?" Jagger exclaimed.

"I need a fucking drink." Kael exhaled as he fell into a chair. Rolling his eyes, Con moved his hand and a bottle of Laphroaig was on the table with several glasses.

"Handy." Jagger pulled the cork out and poured a stiff drink for all three of them and then another for Kael, who downed it in moments.

"He's with the vampires." Kael motioned to Con with a tip of his chin.

"Human, you are a simpleton," Con said good-naturedly, taking a sip of the scotch.

Jagger looked shocked for a moment and then chuckled, motioning for Con to go on.

"I take it you are a hunter too?" Con asked Jagger, who nodded. "Most vampires are not like those you hunt." He patiently explained the Oath to them and that vampires like Anton were Oathbreakers.

Kael continued to look at him with disbelief but Jagger was clearly thinking things over. Con stood up. "I must take my leave. My wife needs me." He hesitated a moment and decided to speak his mind. "Charvez women are special, Kael. It takes a strong man to be with one. They are bright, burning lights that will add to your life immeasurably. There's no escape once you start loving one. You're in it for the long haul. I hope you realize that."

"What the hell are you talking about?" The scotch was working and his words had slurred a bit.

"I saw the way you looked at Simone. Are you a liar as well as an idiot? Simone Charvez is an incredibly beautiful woman. But more than that, she's talented, smart, funny and fiercely loyal. She's more than her looks and she's not to be taken lightly."

"Like I'd touch a woman in the service of vampires. I don't do sloppy seconds."

And suddenly Con's hand was at Kael's throat. "I will tolerate a lot from you, Gardener. I can sense your pain, my wife says you radiate it. But Simone is my family. She is special and you will not speak of my family in such a derogatory way."

With that warning Kael was shoved into a chair and Con disappeared from the room.

"Whoa," Jagger said, watching the empty space that Con had occupied mere seconds before. "You want to tell me what the fuck happened tonight?"

"After you found out that the siren—Simone—was related to the vampire, I went out to look for her. I was circling back to come home when I saw her walking up the street. I grabbed her, pulled her into an alley and demanded an explanation."

Kael pushed a hand through his hair with a sigh. "She was scared and then pissed and Anton showed up with a few of his buddies and attacked us." His face darkened as he remembered her screams of terror. Still, she'd fought so hard, never giving up. His heart ached as he remembered how she'd looked lying on that couch, pale and nearly lifeless from the bite. *Damn it*! He yearned to have her there with him, to touch her and know for sure that she was all right.

He told Jagger the rest of the story until the point where he and Con appeared in the living room and Jagger listened, taking it all in.

Chapter Four

ꟹ

Kael lay in his bed and watched Simone walk toward him. The way she moved was just another sexy thing about her. It was sensual, feline and sinuous.

With a sexy, secretive smile, her graceful hands unbuttoned the front of her dress. First one shoulder was bared, then the other. Her skin was exposed to his gaze inch by inch as the dress came off until she stood there before him in little more than a tiny scrap of lace covering her pussy and a sheer bra of the same ice-blue color. The curve of her breasts mounded above the line of the bra, offering her up like a salacious treat.

Mesmerized, he watched her hands glide up her stomach, over her ribs, to take the weight of her breasts in her hands. He could see the dusky shade of her nipples through the material of the bra. He inhaled swiftly as she reached around and popped the catch. She dipped her shoulders, allowing the straps to fall, and the bra slipped from her body.

Her skin had a deep olive tone, she was nearly golden. Her lips were glistening as her tongue darted out to moisten them.

"You're so beautiful, siren. Let me see all of you," he murmured appreciatively.

"What'll I get if I do?" she asked in a murmur, that catlike smile still on her lips.

He laughed and sat up to see her better. "Oh, I'll make it worth your while, siren. I promise you that."

With a sexy lilt to her lips, she slid her panties down her hips and legs and stepped out of them. She stood there then, naked. She was a goddess. Sexy, voluptuous, curved and soft.

Her legs were long, her breasts heavy, nipples so gorgeous his mouth watered. Her silky hair draped over her shoulders and breasts. His skin wanted to feel its caress.

He pulled the sheet back and she came toward the bed. One knee, then the other on the bed as she joined him. Those breasts of hers swayed deliciously as she moved. When their flesh touched, both of them gasped at the intensity of feeling. He slid his hands into her hair, cradling her skull and pulling her toward him. His lips touched hers and all pretense of gentleness disappeared as they became one, devouring each other in a flurry of lips and hands, of writhing bodies and moans.

When the kiss broke, Simone looked into his eyes. "You have to let go of your pain or you'll never be able to have love."

Kael pulled back from her with a growl and sat up in bed. He looked around, confused and angry. He was alone. Scrubbing his hands over his face, he realized it had been a dream. But her scent was in the air, heavy and lush.

* * * * *

Simone groaned as she came toward consciousness. Her eyes fluttered open and she found herself looking up into her mother's face.

"Simone, *chérie*! You're awake, thank goodness!" Lou exclaimed softly, relief plain in her voice.

Within moments, other faces crowded into view as the gathered members of her family came to her side to assure themselves she was all right.

"Aidan," Simone said quietly.

He came to her and sat down on the bed where she'd been moved after it appeared that Anton wasn't going to stir any trouble. She took his hand. His sorrow, his guilt bled from him.

She kissed his knuckles and smiled softly, shaking her head. "No. All of this is meant to be. Everything that happened in that alley was meant to happen."

Alex laughed softly and pushed the hair back from her forehead. "You witchy Charvez women."

Simone smiled softly. "Aidan, I can feel your guilt. It's not your fault. That thing in the alley was not you."

"He's a vampire, Simone. I should have said something but I hesitated and it nearly cost you your life. He could have killed you."

"But he didn't, Aidan." A tall dark-haired man walked around Aidan and looked down at Simone with a smile. She caught his regard, his attraction and his fierce determination.

"Simone, this is my brother Connor. He's an Oathkeeper. He's here to stop the Oathbreaker."

Connor took her hand and kissed it gently. "And I will. I promise you that. I always get my target. How are you feeling?"

Despite herself, she was charmed by the Irish lilt to his voice and the piercing stare of his deep blue eyes. "Like I was attacked by a vampire in a disgusting alleyway in the French Quarter." She put her hand to her neck where the bandages were. "Did he change me?" Simone tried to keep the fear from her voice but it was there.

"No. He took quite a bit of blood, but you're young and strong and healthy. Con used some healing spells. So did Em and your family. You should be on your feet again within a day or so."

They explained to her about the possibility of her being linked to the vampire and that she'd have to be watchful for any of his emotions leaking through. Simone took it all in, stunned and scared but resolved to see it through.

Em came to sit in the bed next to her, relieved to be feeling her cousin again, even if what she felt was Simone's confusion and fear.

"Kael? Oh god, is he all right?" Simone sat up, alarmed.

Em gently put a hand to her shoulder and pushed Simone back to the pillows. "He's all right. Con saw him home safely. He's a vampire hunter, Minnie." And he was her man. Oh, this was not going to be easy for either of them.

"I know! He came up to me on the street earlier. He was so angry at me. So much pain spilling from him. But I could feel the vampire too, he was coming. Coming for me. I was panicked. And Kael wouldn't listen and he thinks Aidan is like that other vampire. But he protected me anyway. Even when he thought I was bad like them he still protected me."

"That's because he's a good man. He's misinformed about vampires, that much is clear. But he's a good man. He does what's right." Em hesitated for a few moments. "And, well, as he's your mate and all, I suppose we'll all have to get used to him."

"What! He's my what? Oh no he isn't!" Simone exclaimed over the general chaos the statement brought from everyone else in the room.

"Come on, Minnie. I can feel you both. He's drawn to you because he's yours. And you, you'd never take such behavior from any man, much less one with tattoos and piercings all over the place, if he wasn't your man."

"But that's just it. I can feel him too. You can't feel your mate." Simone said, crossing her arms over her chest. Em almost laughed at Simone's attempt at denial. They both knew each other so well.

"You feel his pain. Anything else?"

"What else is there? Pain and rage and not a whole lot else."

"No, there's a lot more. You only feel the pain because he's got so damned much of it. Something so tragic happened to him that he bears deep emotional scars from it. It spills from him in waves. If he weren't so wounded you wouldn't be able to feel him at all."

Lou watched her daughter and felt her pain. Not as an empath feels, but as a mother feels. "What did you feel from him, Em?"

"When he woke up, his first thoughts were of her. Yes, pain. Yes, rage and anger and hurt and defensiveness. But her. He felt protective and tender. The ember of his yearning for her burned deep."

"Oh, they all yearn!" Simone said frustratedly. She waved a hand in Connor's direction. "Hell, that one yearns right now."

Connor coughed and Aidan laughed.

Em looked back at Aidan's brother. "Oh, he wants you. Finds you attractive. Alluring. But they all do that. Even the gay ones like you. Damned annoying growing up with a cousin who looks like you, I'd like to add. Sheesh. A sister who looks like a beautiful doll and a cousin who's a bombshell." Em rolled her eyes good-naturedly and winked at Con. "No, Kael wants more than your bed, Minnie. He wants *you*. He yearns deep for you, to possess you but not to own you, not like that."

"He hates me! He thinks I'm a vampire slut or something. Ugh! A man thinks I'm a groupie. The horror! On top of that he thinks I'm pretty and shallow."

Em felt the pain rip through Simone at that statement despite her attempt at levity. Em narrowed her eyes at her cousins, Simone's brothers, to keep them quiet. "*Bébé*, he doesn't hate you. I felt him. I wouldn't lie about something this important and you know it. He's scared to love. There's loss there. He's built a fortress around his heart and he's terrified to let anyone in lest he lose them. You're the key, Minnie. You're the key to his healing."

"The hell she is! You think we'd let her be with some man who nearly got her killed?" one of Simone's brothers railed.

"There is no *let*. You know how it is with us. He's the other half of her heart. They are made for each other," Lou said softly to her sons.

"*Maman*?" Simone sounded unsure and afraid, and yet there was hope there too.

"*Chère*, when you woke up, you looked up into Aidan's face and you said that everything that happened in that alley was meant to be. It's not always easy, but look inside yourself, you know Em is telling the truth." It pained Lou to say it. She wanted someone stable and safe for her only daughter. She wanted her daughter's love to be easy and free from danger and hardship. But fate handed you exactly what you needed, even if you didn't know it.

Simone closed her eyes against the truth of it. "It doesn't matter. He hates me and I may have a psychic connection to an evil vampire, which will only make him hate me more."

Lee laughed. "Oh, *chère*, I fully expect you to school this boy before he finally gives in to what he feels. But he doesn't hate you. All of his behavior toward you is bluster. Remember that little dog we found back when we were kids? That little scruffy terrier! Oh how he growled and snapped at us when we tried to get close. He'd run in and gobble up the food we left for him. He'd stay around, just outside our reach."

"And I cried to my daddy that the doggie hated us. He picked me up and held me close and told me to look at how the dog shook each time there was a loud noise or anyone spoke loudly. To look at how one of his little eyes was all cloudy and messed up. He said that the dog had probably been abused and that someone had hurt him so bad that he wanted to trust our love but he was afraid to." Simone smiled at the memory.

"And little Sparky did come around. God, you couldn't get that dog out of your lap! *Tante* Elise had that dog forever." Lee laughed.

"So you're saying that Kael is like that messed up little screw-eyed dog? Fleas and all? Snapping at us because he's been hurt so bad?" Simone sighed. "It makes sense, given the general level of pain he puts off. Still, he does make you want to kick him in the junk."

Alex choked back a laugh. "Well, I'm guessing that the education he's going to get will be a detailed one. In the end he'll see that loving a Charvez is worth it." Alex grinned, nuzzling into Lee's neck.

"I almost feel sorry for him. If he wasn't such an arrogant ass, I definitely would," Aidan grumbled.

"Until this fool comes to his senses, I'd like to keep you very close to me, Simone." Connor delivered a devastatingly charming smile. "Not just because you're so beautiful and your voice is like honey. I want you safe."

"Oh, my." Simone fluttered her lashes in his direction. She may have been injured and nearly killed but that surely didn't mean she had to pass up an opportunity to flirt with such a gorgeous specimen. "No sense in putting all my eggs in one basket now is there?"

Connor threw his head back and laughed. "Delightful. I do believe it's been at least a hundred years since I've looked this forward to my job."

"It's a good thing these two aren't meant to be together," Em said in an undertone to Con, who chuckled.

"I heard that," Simone tossed back at her cousin.

"Enough playing, children! Simone needs to rest now," Lou said, a smile playing at the corner of her lips. She tucked the blanket up under Simone's chin. "A lot of magic has been used to heal you, *chère*. I want to get some food into your belly, get you strong again."

"Okay, *Maman*. I need to rest before the shop opens in a few hours and Aidan and Connor will need to get to bed themselves."

"You are not going to the shop today!" Lou rounded on her daughter, hands on her hips.

"I'll open up at two instead of eleven but I'm going to open. Can someone go out there after sunrise and put up a sign saying that? I'll change the shop's voicemail now while I wait for some food."

"Simone Isolde Charvez! Did you hear me?" Lou scolded. "You will not leave this bed for at least another day."

"*Maman,* I have to open. I have customers coming in at three for a fitting and I can't just close down. I'll lose money if I do. I feel much better and I already promised not to leave the building, which is warded tight. I was stupid to leave last night, but I won't do it again."

Lou sighed heavily. Simone's brothers made annoyed sounds but they all knew her well enough to know she was more stubborn and headstrong than any other living Charvez. If she got it into her mind to go to her shop, she'd do it even if she had to do it on her hands and knees.

"We'll make sure someone is with her at all times. There are humans with the Oathkeepers I've brought with me." Connor said this without taking his eyes from Simone.

She nodded slowly, accepting that.

Her *grand-mère* brought up some soup, thick with vegetables and rice and tea. She ate it all under their watchful eyes and fell asleep after forcing Lee to promise they'd wake her at noon.

Connor walked out into the hallway with the others. "I'll set up her guard and then get some rest. I'll go to her myself after the sun goes down. We've got people out asking questions now, trying to find their nest. Perdue will be in a posh setup somewhere, he's not one for empty crypts like most of the rest of them. She'll be all right during the day."

"I'll shimmer her over when it's time. Of course, I'll take the guard over first," Con said.

"That's silly. I'll take one, you take the other," Em said. "Lee will be safe here with a wizard and various and assorted witches and bodyguards."

He sneaked a look at Em. "Sweet, perhaps you should stay here. I don't want you risking yourself. There's no need for it."

She narrowed her eyes at him. "Conchobar MacNessa, I am not a fragile flower. I have your speed and even better magic than you do. Anyway, it'll take thirty seconds to do it all."

He sighed and caught Connor's amused eye. "Aye. Fine. Now let's rest while we can."

* * * * *

Kael spent most of the morning scouring the city for signs of a nest. The problem was that there were fucking vampires all over the place! The casual acceptance of vampires by the paranormal community in New Orleans agitated him. They seemed to live quite openly and no one was afraid of them. The things MacNessa had told him the night before lurked in the back of his brain, but he refused to accept them.

Pulling back into the spot in front of their home, he saw that there was movement in Simone's shop. He turned off the ignition of the motorcycle and looked to Jagger, who shrugged.

"Let's go have a look."

"Mind your manners, Kael. That Faerie wasn't joking last night when he had you by the throat. And maybe you should think hard about what he told you about these Oathbreakers," Jagger said quietly as they crossed the street.

Kael snorted, pushing the door open and seeing his siren glide into view. She had a pretty scarf tied around her neck. He guessed it was to cover the bite mark. He noted her pale skin but was relieved to see that she seemed generally healthy.

When Simone turned they locked eyes and the shock of that connection to one another singed his nerve endings. Damn, if they ever got into bed together they'd bring the roof down. He hardened at the thought. Her scent teased his senses, his blood heated at her nearness.

"Kael, are you all right?" She looked concerned as she moved toward them. The smoky velvet of her voice wrapped around him and squeezed.

"Fine. Your brother-in-law, the Faerie, he did some healing mojo on me and I'm a hundred percent again." He looked at her carefully, saw the lines of strain around her eyes. His fingers itched to smooth over them, to gentle her, take care of her. Unable to stop himself, he allowed a touch of the silky scarf at her neck. "You okay? You were pretty tore up when I left you last night."

She licked her lips and blinked at him. He fell back into the dream for a moment, tasting her on his mouth, feeling her nipples under his palms. He shook his head sharply to dislodge it but the sense of it remained.

"I'm better. I…there…I'm expecting customers but I need to speak with you about all of this. Can you come back after I close? There are some people you need to meet and I think you should share information with each other."

A very large man brought a cup of tea to Simone. She turned to him and gave him a smile so lovely that both Jagger and Kael were nearly felled by it. "Thank you, Max. You're so sweet to me."

The big mass of muscle actually blushed. "Oh, it's no problem, Ms. Charvez. You need to keep your strength up. I promised I'd take care of you."

She patted his arm and he blushed again and blended back into the woodwork. She turned back to them, still smiling. "So can you? Come by?"

Kael, ridiculously jealous of that exchange, snorted. "I'm a busy man. I don't have time for tea and crumpets and sending you simpering looks."

Simone's smile slipped off her face, hurt flashed through her eyes and Jagger smacked the back of Kael's head sharply. The movement caught her eye and she noticed the other man standing there.

She blushed prettily and held out her hand to shake his. "Oh, please excuse my terrible manners. I'm Simone Charvez."

Jagger took her hand and kissed the knuckles. She smelled of magnolias and clean skin. Beneath that he could smell her magic. She was beautiful and charming, but Jagger had a feel for people and she was genuine too.

"I'm Jagger Constantine. I'm a hunter like Kael. Only I have manners." He looked darkly at Kael, who was sullen and pouting. "It sounds like we definitely need to speak with your people. What time shall we come?"

"I close at six. Why don't you come over at six-thirty or so?" She smiled at Jagger, charmed by him. He had pain, but there was a seed of hope there within him. Hope and deep love for Kael Gardener. "I'm sorry but we won't have crumpets. You and Sparky there will just have to make do with iced tea." Simone shot daggers at Kael, amused by her use of the little dog's name, and then smiled back at Jagger.

Jagger chuckled. "We'll be here at half past six, then."

"It was a pleasure meeting you, Jagger," Simone said with Southern honey in her voice. She turned her back to Kael and sauntered toward the two women who'd just entered the shop.

It was like the sun had hidden behind the clouds as her attention went elsewhere. She simply acted as if he didn't exist and it chafed Kael severely. He was tempted to say something but the wall of muscle growled at him and Jagger grabbed his arm, pulling him out of the shop.

* * * * *

"Don't you think you were awfully hard on her?" Jagger said as they got back into their house.

"Did you see how she flirted with the bodyguard?"

"No. I saw her smile and thank someone who did something kind for her. Oh do tell me where the crime is in that? You look at the woman like she's a steak and you're a starving man. Her entire being lit up when you walked in and you talked to her like she was nothing."

"She's vamp leavings, Jagger!" Kael slammed his fist into the wall.

"Stop being an asshole, Kael." Minx spoke from her perch on the counter where she'd sat watching the argument. "Anyway, I thought you said the dude last night said there were different kinds of vamps. That there were good ones and that this Simone was related to a good one?"

"You ever see a good vampire, Minx?"

"No. But I haven't seen a lot of things that exist. Hell, I never saw a Faerie before and lo and behold, one was in our living room last night, apparently. We may have been wrong all this time, Kael. All we've seen are killer vampires, but what if that isn't the whole story?" Minx watched him carefully.

"You two are letting this woman get to you! She's got you in her thrall!" Kael paced.

"Bullshit. I haven't even met this chick. I do know one thing—she gets to you. I can't say I remember a woman ever getting to you like this. You've wanted to kill the female vamps, wanted to fuck your share of women we've met, but this is different. Deeper." Minx watched him as he moved.

"Sure you love us, but this woman, she's under your skin. There's something here, Kael. Don't turn your back on something that could be real." Jagger looked at him with those eyes that saw so much and dared him to argue.

Kael's mouth opened to deny it but he couldn't. Simone Charvez *did* get to him. But he was absolutely sure that once they got into bed a few dozen times, it would wear off. But first this murderous vampire had to be stopped.

He stormed out of the room as Jagger explained to Minx about the meeting.

* * * * *

Simone watched Kael walk across the street after he left the shop, hungrily taking in the way he moved—all leashed menace and threatened violence. She touched the scarf at her neck where his fingers had brushed.

She pushed the hurt away. She didn't have time to deal with it then and more than that, she didn't want to. Instead she put all her attention into her customers until she turned the "closed" sign over at six. Con and Em shimmered into the room with Connor and Aidan.

Em immediately picked up on Simone's distress and they went upstairs to Simone's apartment. Once inside the bedroom, Em shut the door and sat on the bed, watching while Simone changed into flat sandals and a cool pair of white linen capri pants with a deep blue sleeveless blouse. The woman had been nearly killed less than twenty-four hours before and she looked like she'd stepped out of a photo shoot.

"You want to tell me what's wrong?"

Simone growled with frustration as she spun and pulled her hair into a ponytail. "That man! I couldn't have my mate be someone like Connor? Oh no! I get the biggest asshat ever created! Mr. Chip-on-his-shoulder. He's all over the map, Em. One minute he's giving me gentle concerned eyes, asking if I'm all right, looking at me like he'd bend me over something and fuck the hell out of me if he could. The next he's snarling at me and talking to me like I'm dirt."

"Oh, *chère*, I'm sorry. You certainly did get an extra helping of trouble with this one. But there's a reason for it. We can't see it now, but he's for you. You're for him. I'm sorry he's such an idiot." Em stood up and hugged her cousin tight. "If it's any consolation, I'm absolutely sure you're going to make him pay for his abominable behavior."

"While the idea of punishing him for being such an utter prick is attractive, I just hate this. I want to have the kind of love with someone like you have with Con. I want him to moon over me like a lovesick puppy. God, Con looks at you like you're the best thing ever. Like you hung the moon."

Em quirked up a smile. "Yeah, he's a keeper. But don't forget he had his share of prickitude. And let me tell you, what a floozy the man was before he met me. Imagine, ten thousand years of women who are all so very annoyed that he's with me. It's a trial, and you know what a flirt he is."

"I suppose you need to adjust his attitude when he gets out of line, Charvez-style then, hmm, *chérie*?"

Laughing, the two cousins walked out into the apartment. The men seated there looked up at them.

Con watched his wife with a smile, the adoration clear in his face. Em returned the look and sat next to him. He pulled her tight into his body and Simone couldn't hold back a sigh of longing. She wanted that connection.

"The human hunters are here," Max said. Connor stood with Aidan and moved farther into the room. Con's body went on alert, muscles at the ready should trouble break out. Lee rolled her eyes at Em and Simone.

"Puhleeze," Simone said and got up. She pushed past Max and the other vampires who'd come in some moments before and went to greet Kael.

When she got down the stairs she heard the problems starting already and sighed. "Why am I not surprised that you don't play well with others, Mr. Gardener?"

Kael looked up and saw his siren, hands on her hips, eyes narrowed. Her hair was pulled up away from her face and she looked, for want of a better word, lovely and fresh. Even with a bandage on her neck she looked like spring. Her eyes flashed annoyance but that electric connection between them was there as well.

"I'm not walking into a vampire nest unarmed."

"You aren't walking into a vampire nest at all. This is my shop and my home. I am not a vampire, nor do I nest," she said, wrinkling her nose. As if! Nesting? Like some sort of feral animal?

"I'm not coming in there without my weapons," he said through gritted teeth and the humans with him watched the exchange with fascination, mirrored by the various people who'd come from upstairs.

"Are you insulting my hospitality, Sparky?" Simone stalked over toward Kael until she was standing nearly nose to nose with him.

"I'm saying I don't go into a nest without weapons," he repeated.

"Are you slow? Were you dropped on the head as a child or something? This isn't a nest. As if I'd live in something called a nest. I've invited you into my home to share information. You will not bring weapons into my home."

"Then I'm not coming in." He was smug as he said it, crossing his arms over his chest.

Her eyes widened for a moment before she narrowed them again. "Okay." She turned on her heel and walked away. She waved her hand at everyone. "Let's get on with this, he's leaving."

Jagger, Minx, Daniel and Cap looked from the shapely brunette back to Kael, who seemed mesmerized by the sway of her walk and how she'd just essentially told him to fuck off.

One of the big bodyguards walked to the door and opened it, shooting them a look.

"Oh for goodness' sake!" Minx threw up her hands in exasperation. "Wait!" She pulled off her rig and handed it together with the weapons to the bodyguard. "Look, Kael, why not just hear what they have to say?"

"They're vampires, you can't believe anything they say!"

Simone turned back and stomped over to him again. "You are a bigot, Kael Gardener. Someone needs to wash your mouth out with soap. Aidan Bell is an honorable man. I've had it with your temper tantrums. Now if you can't be civil in my home, take your rude butt right back out the door right now. I've assured you that you'll be safe from harm, you have my word. Give your weapons to Max and come upstairs. Time is wasting. It's after dark, he'll be out and about." Simone shivered and looked past them out the windows.

"She's right," Jagger said, handing his weapons to Max. Cap and Daniel did the same.

Simone introduced herself to them and they all followed her upstairs, leaving Kael to grudgingly disarm and follow.

Once Kael walked into the apartment her scent hit him like a fist. Her touch was everywhere. Vibrant colors exploded into view. Lush plants on shelves gave the air a clean, crisp feel. It was an elegant space, sensual, beautiful, like her.

His eyes moved about the room until they landed on her and he frowned. She was standing next to Bell and another vampire. In fact, there were three more vampires in the room and none of them looked too happy to see him.

"Please, sit down," Simone turned to Connor and Aidan, "everyone." They all obeyed and Minx winked at her.

A tray with tall glasses of tea was passed around. Kael gave the evil eye to Jagger and Cap, who seemed to be under his siren's spell, eating her cookies and drinking her tea like this was a fucking tea party.

"Hello..." he started but Simone put her hand up to silence him.

"Don't you start with that." She gave him a narrowed eye that dared him to try. "Now, introductions." Simone introduced the vampires to the hunters. Each side eyed the other warily.

Connor began to fill them in on what they'd found out about Perdue and what they knew about his history and movements.

Simone had stood up to get some more tea when her knees buckled as a wave of evil passed through her. She was dimly aware that someone had caught her and that she was being moved.

Laughter echoed through her head and she used all her strength to wall it out. To reach back to her apartment and push Anton Perdue out of her consciousness.

Kael had been watching her, hands gripping his knees out of sheer desperation. He'd wanted to grab her and kiss her. He'd wanted to smooth his hands over her body to make sure she was whole and unharmed.

She'd been smiling as she walked, listening to something Bell's brother had been saying, when her body seized, eyes rolling up into her head.

Kael was up and over the couch and to her in moments, shoving the vampires out of the way with an inarticulate growl. She felt right in his arms, made to be there. His heart pounded as he felt for her pulse and he relaxed a bit when he found it steady.

"Simone, baby, wake up!" he said urgently, his lips to her ear.

Em knelt quickly across Simone's body from him and Con joined her. "Kael, please, let us help," Em said quietly, touching his arm.

"What's happening to her? Is she epileptic?" Kael's voice was laced with panic as he moved back a little to allow Con access to Simone's body.

"No. Damn it, I was afraid of this," Aidan said as he paced.

Lee and Alex were near the windows holding hands and the room was filled with magic.

"Afraid of what? What have you done to her?" Kael demanded.

"Not me. Anton. When he bit her…a connection was formed," Aidan said, anguished.

"A connection?" Kael wanted to dump Simone's body to the floor and run from the room but his hands wouldn't let go of her.

"Is she his human servant now?" Jagger asked from the couch.

"No! What is it with you guys?" Connor exclaimed. "There are no human servants running around like Renfield from Dracula. A newly turned vampire is susceptible to his Scion's will, yes, like a child is to a parent. But a bite doesn't turn a human into a slave."

"Bullshit! We've seen humans kill for these vampires during the day to protect them!" Minx said, her chin out, eyes blazing.

"You don't have to be a slave to kill, Ms. Rodriquez. Humans kill each other all the time. It's not that they're slaves. Oathbreakers often team up with the human criminal element and reward them with drugs, women, money—what have you—to gain protection during the day. I have human members of my Keeper team, they aren't slaves."

Minx sat back silently as she thought about it.

Simone's eyes fluttered open and she sat up with a sigh. She was essentially perched on Kael's lap and they locked gazes. His hands were around her waist and he held her tight, the softness of her ass and thighs over his. *Oh god*, the heat of her was directly over his cock.

"Simone," was all he could get out before he leaned in and brushed his lips over hers. Even as he did it he was screaming in his head to stop, to back off, but his body had other plans.

Her body melded into his, her arms went around his neck as she clung to him. Her lips were lush and soft and she tasted like the almond cookies they'd been eating before she collapsed.

The world narrowed in focus until all that existed were his lips on hers, her body against his, his arms wrapped around her waist. He took in her breath, her tiny sighs of pleasure as she writhed against him to get closer.

His cock pressed into the softness of her ass, one of her breasts was pressed against his chest while the other teased his arm with each breath and movement of their kiss. He groaned aloud when she opened her mouth under his and her tongue darted out to feather over his lips.

"Kael!"

Kael heard his name being called but tried to ignore it, tried to ignore everything that wasn't this woman in his arms. Her taste surging through him.

She truly was a siren. Her body against his sang a song through his blood, heated it at the same time as he felt an unarguable sense of home. Of rightness.

"Kael! Dude, step back!"

"Simone! Honey, you're in a room filled with people! Minnie!"

One of Simone's hands gently pushed on his chest and she broke the kiss with a soft gasp. Kael looked into her face, into those big golden eyes. Her lips were swollen from his kisses and glistening. She was flushed and her breathing shallow. He couldn't quite believe that a creature so beautiful, so alluring and seductive, was there in his arms, looking up at him like he was the finest thing on the planet. His heart expanded until she filled it completely and settled there.

Kael slowly came back to himself as he heard Con chuckling and Em smack him. *Oh shit!* He'd just laid a lip-lock on a woman in her living room. A room chock full of her relatives.

"I'm sorry," he murmured and set her away from his body. Her eyes, which had only held him with intense desire for long moments, then flashed with embarrassment. She blushed prettily and pulled back into Em.

He stood up and backed off toward the couch, where he collapsed back next to Jagger, who was staring at him like he'd grown a second head.

"Minnie, are you all right?" Em asked Simone.

Simone looked into her cousin's eyes and knew she meant the kiss and not the vampire but she couldn't deal with the kiss right then. "I was walking into the kitchen when I felt him slide into my head. I could feel him like I can feel you, Em. Rage. So much rage and hatred. But it's not hot like Kael's rage. It was cold and deep and it pulled me under." She looked up at Aidan and Connor. "He knew he was in my head. I heard him laughing. Taunting me."

Aidan helped her up and into a chair. Connor pressed a glass of lemonade into her hand. She knew the sugar would help and drank deep.

"Was it hard to drive him out? Or did he leave?" Connor asked, searching her face.

"I pushed him out. It was harder than any other time that I've had to push out someone's emotions. And when someone gets to me, they're always right near me, at least in the same room."

"There's no one here but us. My men are all over the place, stationed around the building and down the street. I've checked in with them. He's doing this long distance through the bite. He has your blood and it's made him stronger too."

Simone took a deep breath. "What are we going to do? Can I use this to find him?"

Kael's heart surged at that. First in admiration of her courage and then in terror that she'd be hurt.

"Well, thank you, darlin', but I'd prefer you to be safe. Even if I didn't adore you, your cousin would kill me if you got any more hurt." Aidan smiled at her and Kael liked the vampire for a few short seconds.

"Why don't we get you into bed, Minnie? Everyone can plan and you can rest." Em stood and held out her hand. Simone snorted at her.

"Oh please! I'm not made of glass! This thing..." Simone hesitated because in truth, first the vampire had nearly killed her and what he'd just done to mind was a violation, an assault. It was Kael's kiss that had pulled her back, the desperation on his face when she'd opened her eyes, the echo of her name on his lips.

"I'm fine and I'm not going anywhere," she said finally, waving everyone off. She'd deal with all the rest of it later.

"Minnie," Em started. Simone knew her cousin could feel her inner turmoil and wanted to help.

"I said—*I'm fine,*" Simone repeated through clenched teeth and Em sighed and shrugged her shoulders.

Connor started to say something but thought better of it. Instead, he pulled out a large map and spread it on the low table. "Okay, so we've pretty much ruled out from the river out about six or seven miles. We don't think he's in the actual city itself. Unlike most Oathbreakers, Anton lives in dwellings and not caves and graveyards. He's been alive so long because he keeps a low profile wherever he is."

"You think he might be out in one of the mansions outside the city?" Con said with alarm.

"I think you might be best off sleeping at Aidan's, for now. We've got men out there now looking." Connor spoke frankly.

Con pulled Em to him tightly, pressing a kiss to the top of her head. "You can use our house as a base of operations out that way if you'd like. I'll continue to help but Em will be staying here in the city." He said it with cutting finality and pointedly ignored Em's glare.

They spoke with Kael's hunters, who agreed to a temporary truce while they hunted Anton.

Simone watched him through her lashes. He was so handsome in a feral way and his eyes were piercing and intense. He was wearing a black T-shirt that stretched over his chest. His muscle lay hard and lean against his body, biceps rock solid. The faded jeans he had on pulled taut over his thighs—not tight, he'd have been hindered by tight jeans. His boots had a heavy sole and Simone thought she'd have wrinkled her nose in horror had any other man been wearing them. Instead, they just fed his bad boy appeal.

His tattoos fascinated her. Each time she looked she found something new she hadn't noticed before. She'd spotted one on the inside of each wrist and one on the back of his neck. Three made a rope around the biceps of his right arm.

He probably drank whiskey from the bottle and smoked too. She wanted to groan in frustration because a part of her found the idea appealing.

She looked at Connor, suave and graceful in his black combat-style pants and shirt. He was tucked in and orderly and he smelled like expensive cologne. He'd probably be excellent in bed too. It was easy enough to see his appeal but she cursed inwardly as she realized he failed to move her even the slightest bit.

Sighing, she looked back at Kael, who'd caught her looking at Connor. He gave her a frown and she rolled her eyes at him and went back to listening to the plans for how everyone would split up territory that night.

Lee, Em and Simone all fussed when they were told to stay back with the other Charvez women. "She's going!" Lee pointed to Minx.

"She's battle trained. She can use just about any type of weapon and she's killed ten vampires," Kael said dismissively.

"I've destroyed a demon lord and a fallen god," Lee said, raising a brow.

Aidan barked out a laugh. "Yes, darlin', you sure did. But you're not trained for hunting. She is. Please, go back home and wait. All of you."

"This is stupid. I've got this connection, we should use it!"

"It's too dangerous! Let the people with proper training do what they do best. Wait here and stay safe." Kael narrowed his eyes and glared, arms across his chest.

Frustration made Simone clench her jaw. It wasn't like she was going out with a gun at her hip or anything but this thing was killing people and they were trying to wrap her in cotton. Taking a centering breath, Simone closed her eyes and found the link to Anton. Reaching, she opened it, bringing a gasp to her lips.

Kael sprang across the room to her and grabbed her shoulders. "Simone! No!"

She opened her eyes moments later and he was still holding on to her. "He's killing someone. Find him. Oh god, find him and kill him before he hurts anyone else." Her voice was flat. The bile of the violence she'd felt was metallic on her tongue.

"You are not to do that again!" Kael hissed at her. "Damn it, you don't know what will happen when you do it. You will not risk yourself like that."

Simone touched his cheek gently for the briefest moment. "You can't tell me what to do, stud boy."

"The hell I can't," he said, turning his face into her palm and kissing it.

"I can see we have some things to work out. You seem to be under the mistaken impression I'm malleable just because I'm pretty."

Kael couldn't stop the grin from breaking over his features. She was a pain in the ass. She was related to a fucking vampire and had some kind of emotional link to another. He was a hunter and she was a woman with deep roots. He had no business even sniffing in her direction, but he wouldn't rest until he'd sunk deep into her, her thighs wrapped tight around his waist.

"Chapter two of this discussion will happen later. Now go to your cousin's house."

"I'm not going there. This is my home. It's warded so that no other vampires but Aidan, Connor and his Keepers can come through the door. I run a business. I'm not running and hiding."

The whole exchange happened in quiet tones and the gathered occupants of the room just stared at the two of them. The hunters watched their fierce leader grinning at someone he'd thought of as an enemy. Moreover, she'd defied him, and they hadn't seen that happen before.

Simone's family watched as she cocked her head and held this tough guy off with one hand.

The heat they put off was impressive. It spilled out and filled the room.

"Minnie, I agree that you should stay at the house. It's huge, you're welcome," Lee said.

"No. Now, you all get going." Simone backed up a step and then moved to Kael again. "Oh, and you had better watch your ass out there." Before he could answer she pressed a quick kiss to his lips and stood back again.

"You'd better not be here when I get back, Simone. Go to your cousin's house," he called back to her as he left.

"Bite me," she called back and turned back to Em and Lee. "What?"

"What was that? Minnie, you sucked face with him on your floor, in front of everyone!" Lee exclaimed.

"Pheromones. Chemistry. Who the heck knows?"

"Come back with us, please," Lee said, reaching out and grabbing Simone's hand.

"No. Lee, my home is safe. I can't hide. I have a business to run. A life. We tried the spell and we know it works. No enemy vamps are getting in here. I'm all right. I need to work. I need to think. Plus, don't think I don't know that Connor left a vamp downstairs, and Max will be back during the day. I have a big order coming due in three days that I have to finish. My workshop is here."

Lee started to argue but Em put her hand up. "Don't. It's as useless as trying to argue with you." She looked back to Simone. "But we will talk about what Anton did to you earlier."

"I can't right now. I'm not saying I won't talk about it. I just can't right now or I'll lose it. Working will make me feel better, help me to think and work through it."

Em narrowed her eyes and the two empaths took each other's measure. "Okay, we'll go *for now*. But will you call if you change your mind or want to talk? We'll come over tomorrow to hang out."

"Of course. Thank you both. I love you." Simone hugged her cousins and minutes later stood alone in her apartment.

Chapter Five

ℰ

She worked, doing fine beadwork on the front of the bodice of a dress until her eyes could no longer focus and her fingers felt like lead. It was nearly four a.m. when she stood up, stretching the kink out of her neck.

A long, hot shower followed and she brushed out her hair and headed to bed. She kept a tight lid on her feelings, not wanting to examine the night too closely and not wanting to risk reaching out for Anton when she was alone.

She curled into her bed and it crashed over her. She'd always taken for granted that she was safe. That her power, her connection to the Charvez women kept her free from threat. Sure she was careful at night. She didn't often walk alone in less than secure neighborhoods but she'd had a pretty charmed existence until the night before. Even when they'd been threatened by the dark mages, and then by a demon itself, she'd believed in the power of her family to protect her.

But the previous night she'd lain on the pavement in an alley and her life's blood had seeped from a wound that would have killed her had she not been a witch and had she not had the talent of a Faerie like Con to heal her.

And Anton had thrust himself into her head earlier and it felt like a violation of her mind. He'd pushed into her emotions and filled her with all that was nasty and vile and had used her.

Hot tears broke from her eyes as her body shook. There was a pounding on her door then and she sat up and went out to the living room. A peek through the viewer showed Kael standing on the other side of the door.

"What?" she asked. Her eyes were red from crying, she didn't want him to see her that way.

"Open the damned door, Simone. You sound funny. Let me in."

"That's sleep! Are you all right?" Her hand was open against the door and she realized that Em was right, she couldn't feel him at all. Not even the pain. Resting her forehead against the door, she finally accepted it. *Damn it.* He had so much power to hurt her and she didn't know if she could stand to be hurt any more right then.

"I'm not telling you anything until you open the door."

What a stubborn ass. Sighing, she wiped her eyes on the sleeve of her robe and opened the door a crack, but he pushed into the room and locked the door behind him.

He backed her against it and looked into her face, searching, and it was clear from his frown that he wasn't happy with what he saw. "You've been crying."

"Are you all right?" Her voice went soft in his presence. She felt caught in the undertow of their chemistry. She smoothed a hand up the wall of his chest and stopped when she felt his nipple ring. Oh good gravy, pierced nipples too! She was drawing the line at dirty drawers. If the man's underwear wasn't clean, mate or not, she was tossing him out on his ass.

"Better now," he murmured. "We didn't find anything. Now, why are you crying?"

"It...I wasn't. I have allergies."

He snorted and picked her up and tossed her over his shoulder. "Where is your bedroom?" he asked as he walked through the apartment.

"What? Put me down!"

"Ah, there it is. Smells good, like you." He shut the door with his foot and put her on the bed.

She looked up at him and would have put up a token protest but he pulled his shirt off and she was speechless. He was gorgeous. Runic tattoos decorated his pecs and his belly. His hard, flat belly. A small silver hoop pierced through each nipple.

He grinned and leaned in, pushing her chin up to close her mouth with a fingertip. "Yeah, I feel the same way every time I look at you. But thanks, siren."

"Siren?" she asked stupidly.

He slid his hands down his stomach and undid his belt and then button and zipper. Her eyes followed the movements, rapt. He sat on the chair near the door, gap in his pants and pulled off those boots. She watched. The socks looked decent enough. That was hopeful at least. He stood in one fluid motion and shucked his jeans and *hallelujah*! the underwear was boxer briefs—her favorite—and in excellent shape.

"What on earth are you smiling at?" he asked. "You haven't even seen my cock yet."

She laughed then and he froze. "Oh, siren, that laugh should be illegal in at least ten states." He stalked to the bed and without any ceremony pushed the underwear down his legs and kicked it to the side.

Her mouth dried up. Oh yeah, so fate might be messing with her, bringing this pain in the butt, but he sure came in a nice package. Or had a nice package. Heh.

"Now," he said in nearly a purr as he leaned down over her, "let's get you naked too."

She nodded earnestly, shrugged out of her robe and tossed her camisole to the side. He grabbed her hands as they moved to push her panties off and stared at her. "God almighty you're beautiful." He pressed his lips to her neck on the side that was free from injury, just over her fluttering pulse. He kissed his way up her neck and over the line of her jaw, his beard tickling the sensitive skin there.

"I suppose you hear that all the time. But I mean it. Damn it, Simone, you do something to me. I shouldn't even be here but I couldn't stay away. Knowing you were up here alone was driving me crazy. I had to see you with my eyes, hear your voice. Smell you." He spoke this in bits and pieces as he kissed around her ears and down her arms and the tip of each finger.

She kept her mouth shut, she was sure all she could manage to say was "glarg" or something similarly articulate. The head of his cock dragged across her hip. It was wet from his arousal and she moaned at the thought of him pushing himself deep inside of her.

"And these," he took the weight of her breasts in his hands, thumbs moving up and over the nipples until she arched into him with a whimper for more. "These are simply unbelievable. Siren, your breasts are spec-fucking-tacular. I thought they were amazing with your clothes on, but these beauties are just made for my hands."

"And your mouth?" she gasped, grabbing him to her.

"Definitely," he agreed as he flicked a tongue over the dusky pink nipple he'd been rolling between his fingers.

Her palms slid over the muscled flesh of his shoulders and back, it rippled with his movement. He was incredibly strong above her, coiled menace, but she felt no fear of him at all. Not physical fear anyway, she knew this man could break her heart quite easily, but it was too late. She loved Kael Gardener, pain and hot abs and all.

The heat of his mouth burned her. Teeth grazed and nipped and his tongue came in to soothe the sting. His hands were strong and sure as they trailed down her body. The sound of the silk ripping brought a gasp from her lips. She caught the flutter of the ripped panties from the corner of her eye as he tossed them to the side.

Skimming her hands down the slope of his back, she stopped when she got to his ass and squeezed. Oh. Yeah, that's the ticket. Hard. She'd gotten a partial glimpse but his pants weren't tight enough. She'd have to get her fill of looking…after they had sex about twenty times.

"Are you an ass woman, Simone?" Kael asked with that grin.

"Not until tonight. But I think you've converted me."

He laughed and she gave a disappointed cry when he moved his mouth from her breasts, that was, until he kissed down her belly.

Her scent drove him wild. He'd never wanted a woman so bad in his entire life. He'd stood outside for half an hour, walking to his own house three times before turning back time and again. He'd argued with himself about her but it was inescapable. He had to see her, make sure she was okay, and then jump those pretty bones.

He settled between her thighs and breathed deep. She was spicy, tantalizing. He parted her with his thumbs and gazed at the glistening pink flesh of her pussy. She was wet and swollen for him.

Her hands touched his face then and he looked up into her eyes and the shock of connection rocked him. He'd felt it before, always had in her presence, it seemed. But there, knowing that they'd make love, it was something truly amazing to experience.

Simone watched as his eyes moved from hers down to her pussy. She should have been embarrassed but she was past that. All she wanted was for him to take her. To lick her and nibble on her, to suck and fuck her into oblivion. Her hormones had taken over and they were not handing back control any time soon.

"Please," she murmured and he obliged with a long lick with the flat of his tongue that sent her hips up to meet his mouth.

The strength of his hands held her hips, tilting her up to his mouth as if he were serving her body to himself. That she could turn inward and submerge herself in the pleasure he was giving with his mouth was an entirely new experience. Usually during sex she had to be extremely careful to keep her partner's emotions out as much as possible. The silence was comforting. It made the experience more her own—it was freeing.

His beard gave slight abrasion in all the right places. She looked down the line of her body and watched the ripple of muscles in his shoulders and forearms as he loved her with his mouth.

Her nipples darkened and hardened. His hair tickled against the softness of her inner thighs.

The swell of her orgasm began to build and she arched with a rough cry when he moved to slide two fingers deep into her. When he hooked them and found her sweet spot she rolled her hips, undulating, riding his hand.

He hummed with pleasure at her taste, at how responsive she was to his touch. Little tremors worked through her muscles, he could feel them in her thighs against his shoulders.

Her breathy moans and pleas for pleasure filled his ears. It wasn't like he was a novice to oral sex or sex at all, but he felt like every other time, every other woman paled in comparison to that moment. To the woman under his mouth and hands. It was so much more than sex and he couldn't find the strength to pretend otherwise, so he gave himself over to it and let himself get dragged under the maelstrom of the way she made him feel.

When he slid a third finger into her, he sucked her clit into his mouth, flicking the underside quickly, relentlessly as he stroked her G-spot.

"Oh my! Yes, please, Kael," she gasped out, hands gripping the pale blond silk of his hair, holding him to her.

It was so good that she wanted to pull away from him completely and yet push herself into his face. Climax tingled at her toes and scalp and suddenly broke through her, filling her body with intense pleasure.

Kael kept his mouth on her pussy, pushing her into an aftershock orgasm on the heels of the first major tremblor. Kept lapping at her like a starving man. And he was. He needed her with such desperate power that he wasn't sure he could survive it. He wanted her so much that his stomach clenched.

"Kael," Simone gasped, trembling with the delicious sensation of her orgasm. She clamped her lips closed before she told him she loved him. She tried to move away and his mouth gentled, pace slowing.

As the last of her orgasm faded, her muscles relaxed and her thighs fell open and hit the bed. She cradled his head between her hands and he finally pulled back, pressing soft kisses to the crease where thigh met body.

She was mesmerized. She watched as he traced her nipple with the fingers he'd had inside her and licked over the glistening tip. It was so intensely naughty that she gasped in reaction to his raw enjoyment of her body.

"Oh, siren, you taste so damned good. I've never tasted anything like it before," he murmured, his mouth around her nipple, eyes rolled up to meet her gaze.

She should have something witty to say but he struck her speechless. A fact that amazed her as much as it scared the hell out of her.

Instead she pushed him onto his back and scrambled over his body. "That's more like it," she purred, whipping her hair across his bare chest and neck.

"I'm all yours, siren. Do with me what you will," he said, a smile on his lips.

She leaned down and left a trail of kisses across his brow, down his temples and over the line of his jaw. She nipped his lip between her teeth and thrilled when he arched into her with a groan. Tasting herself on his lips, she slid her tongue along his, sensuous, slow. She meant to take her time with him. To take tiny bites of him until she was so full she couldn't bear to take another.

His palms skimmed up her thighs and around her, the tips of his fingers drifting up and down her spine.

She moved down a bit so that her pussy was directly above the ridge of his cock and couldn't resist sliding herself over him, grinding a bit while she kissed down his neck and found one of his nipples.

"Simone, you're playing with fire," he warned and she looked up at him with those big golden eyes and he caught a glimpse of the pink of her tongue when it darted out to lick over his nipple.

She tasted salt and skin and hard, hot man. He was deliriously delicious and she hummed in delight when she took his nipple, ring and all, between her teeth and tugged gently.

His hands tightened on her back. "Oh yeah, that's it, siren," he groaned.

She tortured him with lips and teeth on his nipples for a while before she dragged her tongue down each ridge of muscle on his abdomen.

Kael made a desperate sound and took hold of her shoulders, pushing her down. "Why, what is it you're trying to say?" Simone said in her best Southern belle voice, fluttering her lashes at him.

"Siren, either suck my cock or fuck me. I'm at the edge of my patience," he said through clenched teeth. "Holy shit," he hissed out when she obliged, taking him into her mouth.

His cock was hard, veins throbbing beneath her tongue as she enveloped him in her mouth. He was thick and she couldn't wait to feel him inside her. His elemental scent filled her senses. His skin was hot and so very soft.

She moved over him, learning him, what he liked, what made him moan and jerk. What made him tighten his hands on her shoulders. He'd taken great care to not touch near the bandages on her neck. That he was so gentle even when they were drowning in each other touched her deeply.

Simone loved giving head, but not having had a regular relationship very often, she didn't get to do it as often as she liked. She felt like a glutton and nearly laughed at the image.

His thighs were hard beneath her palms, the play of muscles was enticing. Trailing her tongue down the shaft, she pushed his thighs open wide and kissed and licked his balls until he was nearly sobbing with the pleasure of it. A mischievous smile on her face, she kissed back up the stalk of him and, eyes locked with his, licked her way around the ridge of his cock head, dipping the tip into the slit, which was slick with pre-cum. His taste was salty and tangy and unique. Like him. Her blood hummed.

Her mouth was wet and hot and her tongue slid around his cock and the head with a slick, dreamy rhythm. His balls pulled tight against his body. He wanted her so very much that his teeth hurt. Her beautiful hair played peekaboo with her face and trailed across his lower stomach and thighs as she moved up and down on him.

She was on her hands and knees so her ass swayed from side to side in an alluring dance. And what an ass it was. She'd so often worn dresses that he hadn't noticed how tasty it was until earlier that night when he saw her in those white pants. She had the perfect butt for those boy short panties. Round and high, the perfect slice of cheek showing. *Shit*, he was really close to coming.

"Siren, Jesus, siren, stop. I want to be inside of you. Please."

She pulled her mouth off his cock with a slight pop and looked up at him, lips tantalizingly wet and red. "But why?" Such a pretty pout on those lips, he laughed.

"I'm close and I want to be buried deep inside of you. Ride me, Simone. I want to look up at you as I'm deep inside.

I've seen so much ugliness, I want you to wash it away." That was said in a breathless rush, as if his emotions knew his brain would try and stop him from saying it. He bit his bottom lip and she nodded.

She moved up his body, pressing a kiss to his lips as she reached into her bedside table and pulled out a foil packet that she tore open with her teeth and quickly rolled on him. For a brief moment he was annoyed that she had condoms in her bedroom but that was all forgotten as she guided him true and slowly sank onto his cock. She was maddeningly tight.

"Oooooh. Mmmmm yesss," she hissed as her ass met his thighs and he was in to the root.

"Oh, siren. You feel so fucking good," he whispered as she looked down, her hair sliding over her shoulders and draping over her breasts.

"Not half as good as you do, stud boy."

He barked a laugh which turned strangled as she undulated her body on his. Her hard rolling movements kept him seated deep but she rippled around him, her body gripping his in that silky heat.

His hands moved up until he found her breasts and took them in his hands. Her nipples stabbed into his palms. Her breasts were like the rest of her, lush, curvy, sexy. She was like a vision above him, the light from the small lamp was on behind her, lighting a corona around her body, making her skin glow with it.

She arched her back, bent backwards, her hands on his thighs. Her breasts were offered to his eyes and hands, pussy clenching around him as he slid inside deeper than he'd thought he could.

She was wet and hot against him and one of his hands found her clit and slowly circled it while she moved over his body. Each grinding move she made over him pressed her into his fingers and she gasped at the contact. Over and over she moved and gasped.

Gods, he was close and so was she if the way her pussy was fluttering and clenching around his cock was any indicator. "Simone, come for me, gorgeous. I want you to give me one more," he said softly and her head fell back as she ground into him harder and harder, faster and faster.

A groan from deep inside her burst from her lips when he pinched her clit between slippery fingers, plumping it gently. Her nails dug into his thighs as a flush worked up her body. She was juicy and clenching around him until he couldn't take another moment, and moving his free hand to her hip, held her down as he surged up.

The orgasm she'd been keeping him dancing on the edge of for the last hour shot out of him. He felt like the entire universe came from the head of his cock as he thrust deep into her. He whispered her name over and over as the waves of pleasure rocked him, drowned him in sensation. It felt like he came for ten minutes, each time he thought it was over she'd move a little or whimper and it would build again.

Finally, with a long, sated sigh, he fell back against the mattress and she collapsed forward onto his chest.

He moved her to the bed gently and quickly disposed of the condom. She pulled the blanket back and patted next to her body and he slid into bed, turning to face her.

She was incredible then, hair a wild tousle around her face and shoulders, lips swollen, glistening with a sheen of perspiration from her exertions on him. Her eyes glittered in the low light of the room as the sun began to rise.

"Will you stay?" she asked sleepily, putting her head on his arm and looking up into his face.

"Of course." And he would. For the time being. He'd have to be on his way again once this Anton situation was squared away but until then he'd get his fill of her to dull the ache of need he had where she was concerned.

"How did you get in, anyway?"

Her sleepy murmur was even sexier than her smoky purr and his cock twitched as it thought about reviving. The room smelled like sex—like her body and his. It hung in the air around them.

"Max let me in on the vampire's orders." It still burned him to be working with vampires instead of killing them, but he had to admit that their information seemed on the up and up. The more Jagger looked into the information Connor and Aidan had given them, the more it appeared that they'd been telling the truth about there being law-abiding vampires and these Oathbreakers.

It didn't mean he had to like vampires any more than he already did, though. So he just wouldn't kill all of them. There was a brief twinge as he wondered if they'd ever killed an innocent vampire, but as they'd tracked these bands of murderous ones, Jagger and Minx both had assured him that they hadn't. It was too late to worry about at that stage anyway.

"You still don't like Aidan. Even after he saved your life. Saved my life."

"I've spent fifteen years hunting and killing vampires, Simone. I just can't suddenly start seeing them differently."

"You want to tell me why you hate them so much?"

"No. I want to sleep. I hunted vermin all night long and pleasured a goddess, I need rest."

She gave him a ghost of a smile and allowed him to pull her close. It was Sunday, the shop was closed and she was exhausted. He was safe, she assumed everyone else was too or she'd have been called, or hopefully Kael would have said something. His heart beat steadily under her ear, his skin was warm and smelled of him and of her too. She liked that.

* * * * *

Some miles away in his posh mansion, Anton Perdue settled to sleep in his big bed. He had a female tucked on each side of his body and the curtains around the bed and over the windows drawn tight.

The blood of his victims fed his system as their terror had. He was still slightly intoxicated with it.

He thought briefly about the news that Keepers were in New Orleans along with the human hunters and dismissed it with a small thrill. He was more powerful than Keepers, the trained doggies of vampirekind, and certainly more powerful than any human.

He chuckled quietly thinking about the link he'd created with the witch. Her blood had been strong and still fueled him. As Oathbreakers they had less magic than other vampires, but the deaths and her magic-tinged blood had boosted his magical ability and thrall immensely.

Those Bell pups would suffer greatly before he killed them, and the witch would watch. Oh he had plans for the pretty bitch. He reached up to touch the place on his face where she'd gashed him open with her shoe. She had fire, that one did. Yes, he'd take her and feed on her for a while. She was certainly quite something to look at. He hadn't had a female at his side as a regular thing in two hundred years. Perhaps this Charvez witch would make an excellent vampire.

Ah, yes. That was quite an idea. Harnessing her power to make it his own. Turning her and watching her feed. Not just off of blood but emotions. With him as her Scion, he'd be able to use her power as an empath to feed off the emotions she picked up. It'd be a gluttonous feast every night.

A smile on his face, he slid off into his deep day sleep.

* * * * *

Simone sat bolt upright in her bed with a gasp, heart thundering in her chest. She choked back the unease and the terror and when her eyes cleared and she could hear again, she saw Kael before her, his hands holding her upper arms.

"Siren! What is it?" he demanded urgently.

"A dream. I think. He…I…" she dissolved into tears as she realized that Anton had stolen into her mind yet again. She felt violated and threatened.

"Anton?"

She nodded as she cried, hating herself for being so weak but being oh-so glad he was there right then. Grateful that his hands were on her, holding her and stopping her from slipping away.

Kael pulled her into his arms and rocked her, smoothing a hand over her hair. "Shhh, siren. It's over. He isn't here. The sun is up. You're safe with me. I won't let him hurt you, baby."

His words soothed and excited at the same time. She fell another notch for him. Such a ferocity and tenderness for her—to her. Nodding and cutting off a sob as ruthlessly as she could, she nuzzled her face into his neck and breathed him in like a drug.

"Do you want to talk about it?" he murmured into her hair.

"He wants to keep me. Make me into one of them. Oh god, I'd kill people for fun and feed off them and he'd feed off me!" She gasped as the enormity of it hit.

He pulled her back from his body, those piercing blue eyes locking with hers. "You wouldn't be able to help yourself. But I won't let that happen to you, Simone. I wouldn't let you devolve into one of them."

"Promise you'll kill me if he tries to change me," she whispered, knowing what she was asking but needing his promise anyway.

He sighed. "You don't know what you're asking me to do, Simone."

"Yes I do! I can't be that. Lost to everyone I love. Worse—a *threat* to everyone I love! He'd use me, use my magic. I can't. Please promise me you won't let that happen, even if you have to kill me before I change."

He was very still for a moment and then he nodded and pulled her down to the mattress beneath him. "I promise. But you're mine, siren. You belong to me and no one else. He can't have you."

Simone nodded her head, wrapping her thighs around his waist, opening to him.

"Please tell me you have more condoms," he said through clenched teeth.

She nearly knocked over the lamp as she reached up and into the drawer, rifling blind to find one and sighing with relief when she held up the foil packet. He gave a relieved growl in his throat as he opened it and sheathed himself in record time.

She was wet and ready for him and her slickness made that initial thrust into her deep and fast.

"I need you to fuck me, Kael. Make the bad guys go away."

"My pleasure, siren, my pleasure. God, you feel so fucking good," he said as he steadily thrust into her heat. He loved the feel of her silky thighs around his waist, the way she welcomed his cock with the roll of her hips.

Her breasts moved as he fucked into her and her lips were parted, her eyes half lidded. She received him then, took what he gave and returned her own passion to him. A circuit formed, sparks flew, and there was nothing in the world but the two of them—united, seeking pleasure and giving it back.

She felt perfect beneath him, the cradle of her thighs held him. Her fingers combed through his hair and over his shoulders with a featherlight touch. He was battle hard and combat ready and she was soft and perfumed. Her mind was sharp and her tongue quick, he admired that. She was the light to his darkness and he refused to even contemplate what that might mean to a vampire as far gone as Anton Perdue.

Simone Charvez was his as he was hers. No one else would ever touch him the way she did. He mourned a little as they reached orgasm, knowing that no other woman would ever make him feel that way again.

Chapter Six

ꟹ

When Simone awoke sometime after noon, Kael had gone. She rolled over, got out of bed and shuffled into the bathroom.

"He'd better be out getting me some breakfast," she grumbled as she stepped under the water.

When she got out some minutes later, she pulled her hair into a simple knot at the base of her neck and pulled on some light clothes, leaving off the shoes. She frowned down at her toes when she saw how badly she needed a pedicure. Her nails were a mess too.

Her apartment was empty and there was a one line note from Kael on the kitchen table that thanked her for the morning and said he'd be in touch later. She frowned and then shrugged. At least the man left a note. But if they were going to make their relationship work, he'd need to develop some manners.

She picked up the phone and called Lee's.

"Hello?"

"Hey, Em. You and Red fancy grabbing a manicure and pedicure with me? It's still full daylight."

"Simone! Only you would want to get a mani-pedi at a time like this," Em said, laughing.

"Look, just because the world is under threat *yet again* is no excuse to start looking like hell. My nails are chipped from that night in the alley and my toes are equally thrashed. In case you hadn't noticed, it's sandal season!"

"Fine! It's been a while since I got my nails done. It'll give us something to do until dark when they all go off again. Con is out there now, tracking." Em sighed and suddenly was standing in Simone's kitchen with Lee.

Simone looked up and laughed. "Hey, y'all. I know they'll be able to fit us in. Let's get on it. Max is downstairs, we need to bring him with us or we'll get creamed by the guys."

They tromped downstairs and saw that Max was there with Jagger.

"Morning, boys," Simone said. "Have you eaten yet, Max? I know you slept in the back room even though you are more than welcome upstairs in my guestroom. There's food in the kitchen down here but I don't want you starving yourself because you won't leave."

"Yes, ma'am. I had a nice breakfast some time ago, and even a snack. I was getting hungry again, though."

"Hello, Jagger, what are you doing here?" Simone asked.

"Kael wanted me to keep an eye out for you. I hope you don't mind."

"Well, and Kael is where?"

"He had some errands to run. Ammo to deal with. We make our own silver bullets, you know, and we need graphite."

"Uh, no. I didn't know that. Can I watch?" *Cool beans, silver bullets*!

"It's kind of complicated, I don't know…"

"Oh I see, I must be stupid."

"Oh, I never said that!"

"No, but you felt it. Never mind. Max, can you please escort us up the road a piece to my nail shop?" Simone turned her back on Jagger, cutting him off. She was seething inside. He reached out to touch her, to try and apologize, but Em grabbed his hand, giving a hard shake of her head.

"You're getting your nails done? At a time like this?" Max tried not to look incredulous, he didn't want the same treatment Jagger had gotten.

"We're blowing off steam and keeping ourselves up. It's full daylight. Anton is at rest, I can feel that. It's just a few blocks and we're three powerful witches and you're a giant mass of fists."

Max sighed as he looked down into her smiling face. "Okay, let's go. I'll talk to one of the other men. They've been watching the streets around here. We'll get one man per each one of you."

Soon they were walking, flanked and shielded by three of Connor's men, and Jagger had insisted on coming as well. The ladies in the nail shop tittered and fluttered their eyelashes at the gorgeous men who ate up the attention but kept their eyes peeled for any sign of danger.

Once they were seated at three adjoining tables and their nails were being soaked and filed and painted, Em looked over at Simone with a smirk. "So. Consummation."

Lee giggled and Simone laughed. "Can't hide anything from you, Em. Never could."

The men all tried to pretend not to hear but Simone could tell they were listening avidly, including Jagger.

"And? How was it?"

"You've seen the man. What do you think?"

Em laughed. "That good, huh?"

"Oh yeah. My god, the stamina! His body is hard and hot and his abdomen actually *ripples* when he uh," she looked around and lowered her voice, "thrusts. And his nipples are pierced and he's got protective runic tattoos all over his body. They're beautiful but there's a sad story linked to them, that much I can tell."

"And what's the beard like? You know, when he, that is, did he..." Lee blushed.

"It adds a bit of sensation, not too much, just enough to be entertaining. I definitely think one of your men should grow a beard."

They all three laughed and continued to speak in low tones. The men looked at each other briefly and then pointedly avoided eye contact.

An hour later they were walking back through the summer heat and Simone was glad it was just a few blocks. She approached her shop and saw the house across the street and caught Jagger's eye.

"Is that Kael's motorcycle?"

"Yeah, he's back now. I'll call him when we get back to let him know you're home safely."

Simone turned to her cousins and hugged them both. "I'll come over tonight. Con said he'd come for me at sundown. Thanks for hanging out with me for a few hours. I feel better."

"You know we're always here for you. I know this can't be easy for you. Any of it," Em said. "I know he's difficult. But I also know how he feels about you."

"Yes. But he doesn't *want* to feel that way about me. He doesn't want to love me."

"And you don't want to love him either."

"Oh, don't start making me be logical, Em Charvez! He left before I woke up, I hate that! And anyway, maybe I'd want to love him if he wanted to love me back."

"There's no question he needs manners, Minnie. But he's your mate, that's what fate has decreed. I got the arrogant Faerie, Lee got a double helping of male ego and you got this one. But you can't say you'd want it any other way and neither can we."

"Con adores you, Em. Alex and Aidan were blotto over Lee from the moment they saw her. He does not adore me. He thinks I'm a pretty piece of fluff."

"I know you hate that, Minnie. And I can't blame you. He'll learn and most likely the hard way. But you've never had to struggle once in your life to get a man's attention. This will be a learning experience for you too. You have had it easy, they all worship you like puppies. This one is not to be managed like those others." Lee raised a brow and a corner of her mouth lifted.

"Fine! See if I let either of you borrow my shoes from now on!" Simone huffed and then laughed before her cousins shimmered out of sight to go back home.

"We're going over there," Simone called out as she crossed the street and headed to Kael's front door.

Minx saw her coming and waved. "Hey there, Simone. You look like you could use a glass of something cold." She held the door open for her and the bodyguards and ignored Jagger's glower.

"Go on through there. Kael is getting ready to make the bullets. I'll bring the tea through when I get it," Minx called out and Simone winked at her and charged through the doors into the next room.

There Kael worked. The room was hot. The air conditioning was on but it couldn't overcome the heat of whatever it took to heat silver. He had on one of those long aprons they wore in labs when working with chemicals or high temperatures—*most likely some sort of flameproof material,* Simone thought.

"So, do you normally fuck and run, Kael Gardener?" Simone said as she approached him. He looked up sharply in surprise.

"I'm busy. I had stuff to do. I left you a note. It's more than I usually do." He was angry that the mere sight of her clenched his gut and made him want to smile. He was a damned killing machine for fuck's sake! Not some lovesick moron.

Simone put a hand to her chest dramatically. "Oh, why thank you, kind sir! What small consolation it is indeed to get *more than you usually* give to the women you fuck indiscriminately." The last was said through clenched teeth.

Nervousness edged his gut. She was mad, he could see that, and it obviously had something to do with his leaving without saying goodbye. But she'd been sleeping and she needed her rest and he hadn't wanted to disturb her. Hell, he had been disturbed enough when he'd woken up and wanted to take her again. He'd wanted to lounge with her and eat a leisurely breakfast and stay in bed all day. The panic hit him and he'd had to leave.

"I had stuff to do," he repeated and went back to his work.

She stomped toward him and turned her head, looking at the gauge. "It's nearly two thousand degrees, you should be ready to pour it in the molds soon."

He lifted a brow at her.

"What, you thought I only knew about fabric and nail polish?"

"I didn't think anything. What do you know about silver bullets anyway?"

"Not much. I know from Aidan that they have more stopping power with vampires than traditional lead bullets. I know that silver melts at just under eighteen hundred degrees. I took chemistry, you know. Got an A. Do you have special molds? It seems to me that regular molds couldn't take temps this high."

"At first we used jeweler's molds but that required a new plaster mold for every bullet. Costly and difficult to have in supplies if we were out of a city for a long period of time. So I made a set out of graphite."

"Oh, I bet the bullets come out shiny that way."

He looked at her, trying desperately not to show his amusement. He got out the blowtorch and preheated the molds. "I couldn't say. I just kill vampires with them. I have more to worry about than how shiny my bullets are," he said as he poured the liquid silver into the molds.

"You know, you have a severe manners problem. As in, you have none!"

"What do you want, a thank you? Thanks for the great sex, Simone. It was wonderful. Is that what you wanted?"

She recoiled as if he'd physically struck her. "Do you kiss your momma with that mouth, Kael Gardener? 'Cause my momma would smack you upside your pea-brained head for such talk." Her invective spun into French and he just stood there in the face of her wrath. Worse, she looked so fucking beautiful in her anger that he longed to rain a thousand tiny kisses over her face in admiration and to calm her down. But before he did anything stupid she made a disgusted sound, threw her hands up in the air, spun on her heel and stormed out of the room, nearly knocking Minx over before she hurtled out the front door, the bodyguards following quickly.

Minx stomped into the room. "What did you do?"

"Why is it my fault?" Kael asked, looking miserable.

"She looked furious and on the verge of tears. What on earth did you say to her?"

"She was crying?"

Minx blinked at him in disbelief. "I didn't know how I'd feel about her at first. But I like Simone Charvez. What's more, I thought you did too."

"I have too much work to do," Kael mumbled and turned back to the crucible where he had been heating the silver, and worked through the next batch.

*****

Simone slammed back into the shop and went directly into her workroom and began to sew.

Max sent the others back to work and one to get them some takeout. He sat down in a comfortable chair and watched her. "You want to talk about it?"

"That's very sweet of you, Max. But there's nothing to say. Fate sucks. And this time fate is wrong. That man is not my anything."

"Fate is fate, Simone. You can't argue with her. She has things in mind that you just can't see right now. But I've seen the way he looks at you. I watched him last night when they all got back from hunting. He stood out there on the street, looking up at your windows. Finally he swallowed his pride and asked me to let him in."

"How is it a blow to his pride to see me? Am I so awful that it's actually a *knock* to his pride to simply come to me?"

"No, of course not and you know it. But he hates vampires. You're related to one. He has to work with them to find this Oathbreaker. This chafes his pride. And he had to ask permission to come inside. Had to ask *Connor's* permission. Come on Simone, you can see it now, can't you?"

"Why does he hate vampires? I asked him about it last night but he wouldn't talk about it. How can we be together if he won't even talk to me?"

"He'll tell you when he's ready. There's obviously a story there. Give him time. You don't know what I'd give to find my mate. Don't blow this off, you're so blessed to have it. Even if he is an arrogant asshole."

Simone laughed and waved him away. "Thanks for listening. I've got to finish this before I go over to Lee's tonight. Go on. Let me know when the food gets here."

He stood up and blew a kiss her way and sauntered out.

She ate a late lunch and got back to work until nightfall, when Con showed up and took her back to Lee's. The rest would meet them there for a strategy session. Simone took a bag just in case she ended up sleeping over.

Em took one look at her when they shimmered into the room and grabbed her hand. She and Lee dragged her into the front parlor and pushed her into a chair.

"Spill."

"What if I don't want to talk about it?"

"Puhleeze. Try leaving here without telling me why you're so sad. You won't get three feet," Em said as she handed Simone the drink she'd poured.

"He's such a jerk!" Simone told them about what he'd said that afternoon.

Lee rolled her eyes. "This guy is such a dick!"

"No he isn't. Not really. He's scared. Scared of feeling something so deep for anyone he could lose," Em said, sitting on the couch and tucking her feet beneath her. "*Chère,* he's so wounded. He's...I don't know if I have the words. Clearly he loves you. I want to say that up front. I can feel that each time I see him. But he's got an ache, a soul-deep ache. He's lost people he's loved and that makes him afraid to love again. But he's got so much love there that he keeps bottled up. Just give him a chance."

"And how much shit is she supposed to take before he wises up?" Lee said angrily.

"You heard Simone talking about how he treated her when she had the dream about the Oathbreaker. How he was gentle when he made love to her. He's conflicted. He doesn't want to hurt her but he doesn't know how to let anyone in. She scares him."

"*Hello,* I'm in the room!" Simone exclaimed. "I don't want to love him. I don't want this man." She began to pace. "I want a nice man with a good job. A man who can tell me he loves me. A man who doesn't kill things bigger than spiders!" She flopped down again and put her face in her hands. "But damn it, I do love him. I want to heal him. I want to show him that loving me is worth it. I want him to believe I'm worth it. And I hate that!"

Em laughed. "Oh, *chère*, you've never had to work for a man before, have you?"

Simone sighed and shook her head.

"Well, you know what *Grand-mère* says, nothing worth having is easy. I almost lost Con. Lee had to fight off a fallen god and a demon lord to have her loves. Clearly, you are meant to heal Kael. Fate has put you in his path to mend his broken heart. You're humble about your gift and your talent with a needle but you've always been sure about your allure as a woman. Use that." Em kissed her cheek.

"They're here," Lee said from the doorway.

"He's not getting back into my bed until he's made major reparations to me about this afternoon," Simone grumbled.

"Of course! That's how it should be. I said you'd heal him, I didn't say you shouldn't make him crawl," Em said with a laugh as they all walked out into the foyer.

Of course, that was hard to remember when she caught sight of him walking into the dining room.

Minx saw her and approached. "Hi, Simone. I'm sorry about earlier."

"It's not your fault. You have nothing to be sorry about," Simone said with a shrug.

Minx sighed. "There's so much you don't know."

"All he has to do is tell me. All anyone has to do is tell me. I've done nothing wrong here. I've put up with his rudeness and his abrasive bullshit. But I won't take anyone treating me like a whore. Not ever."

Minx reached out and squeezed her arm. "Of course. You shouldn't. And I wish I could tell you. But it's not my story to tell."

"What about your story?"

"That I can tell you. Not now, we're supposed to be working on tonight's plan and Connor is waiting."

Simone suddenly smiled. "Oh! You're sweet on him."

Minx blushed. "Don't say anything!"

"I won't. You're a lucky girl. He's a good man. Handsome, smart, accomplished. Not an ass."

Minx laughed. Kael poked his head out of the room they'd been meeting in, starting when he saw Simone standing there. He searched her face, loving every inch of it. His heart ached knowing that he'd made her upset earlier. He had to make amends, especially before he left town.

"Minx, we're all waiting."

"Keep your shirt on. I'm coming." Minx walked toward the door and looked back over her shoulder at Simone and winked.

Kael put his arm out to stop Simone as she tried to enter the room. "Simone, don't go trying to channel Anton tonight. It's too dangerous."

She would have yelled at him for telling her what to do but she could see his worry for her clear on his face. Still pissed off at him but still in love with him, she sighed. "Listen, everything I do in this house is safe. I'm not going to risk myself unnecessarily, but the fact is that I can use this to find him and the longer we wait, the more people get hurt. I'm a protector of the innocent, Kael. I can't turn my back on that because it's hard."

He opened his mouth to argue but closed it instead and motioned her into the room, where she sat down at the table next to Alex.

The Charvez witches sat in that room—Simone, Em, Lee, Lou and Marie and the matriarch, Isolde. Together they emanated so much power it nearly hummed. Simone drew energy and reassurance from it.

"Okay, we know that three humans went missing last night from Kenner. A family," Connor hesitated a moment and the burst of pain from Kael was so strong that moment that it made Simone slightly nauseated. Her eyes flicked up and she met Jagger's gaze and felt his pain as well. *He'd lost his family to vampires.*

She put her fingers over her eyes for a moment. "We have to stop this. Let me hone in on him."

"It's too dangerous, Simone!" Aidan said from across the table.

"Look, Lee can fight demons and dark mages. Em can fight dark Fae and demon lords. I can do this! I know you all think I'm just a pretty fragile flower but I am a powerful empath and we've got this damned link. Not using it is just stupid."

Em closed her eyes for a moment and Con squeezed her hand.

"No one thinks that, Simone. You're just not battle ready," Connor said reasonably.

"I'm an empath, Connor. Don't tell me lies, I can taste lies." She waved it away with her hand. "Never mind that now. How many children is this vampire going to kill before we accept that this link can be used to stop him? How many times is he going to steal into my head and terrorize me? Huh?"

"Simone, this is about doing things safely. We're not going to risk you like this." Kael's chin jutted forward.

"Oh fuck you all! You don't get to decide. I decide my own fate."

The room got still from shock. Simone was saucy and sexy, she was high maintenance and pretty. She was smart and compassionate. She did not tell people to fuck off.

"That's right, you heard me. If this link existed between Anton and Aidan do you think this would be an issue? No, you'd have used it already. Well, the Compact binds me too, I'll have you know. Things happen for a reason. I have this link with him for a reason. We can't not use it. There are children out there who still think monsters aren't real. We can't fail them, not when we have a tool to stop him."

"Give us another night to hunt him. Then if we haven't found him, you can open the link tomorrow," Connor said.

"I'm opening this damned link tonight. With you all here, or without you. I will not sit by while children are being terrorized on my watch." She crossed her arms over her chest.

"She's right," Con said and Em smiled at him.

"I agree. We're the holders of the Compact. It's our responsibility, our duty. Simone was stricken with this bite, making her susceptible to this vampire. If he can get into her mind, she can get into his." Em locked eyes with Simone and walked over, grabbing her hand. The cousins united. Lee came forward and put her hand on Em's shoulder. Lou, Marie and *Grand-mère* joined the group and the magic crackled. It was almost as if the room expanded, taking a deep breath as their connection filled it.

Aidan put his face in his hands and sighed. Kael looked at the women in disbelief and then back to Connor and Aidan. "You can't mean to let this go forward! Do you know what will happen if this vampire takes her?"

"He won't. Lee and I will link with her. My mother, aunt and *grand-mère* will guard the circle. We've faced far stronger threats than this vampire, Kael," Em said. She could feel the intensity of his need to protect her, to protect his mate. But it had to happen. Simone had to do this, to take control back and to live up to her responsibility as a Compact holder. There was no other way to do it and be honorable.

"I can't sign onto this! This is insanity! Damn it, Simone. Can I speak to you privately?" Kael asked, standing up and holding out his hand.

Simone nodded and went to the door, ignoring his hand.

Kael glowered at the rest of the people in the room and went out into the hall, where Simone was sitting on one of the ornate benches, her long legs crossed, a foot idly swinging back and forth.

"Simone, siren, don't do this to prove something," he said softly, coming to sit next to her.

Staring into his eyes, Simone held her hands clenched in her lap to keep from touching him. "Kael, if you think this is about proving something, we're even worse off than I thought originally." She searched his face. "This is about duty. Plain and simple. You have your duty. Whatever happened to you has made you take up this crusade. But my powers are gifted to me in exchange for me using them to help when necessary. And it is necessary."

"I'm a fighter! Simone, I have been trained to fight and kill vampires since I was six years old. I don't know anything else. But you do. You're soft and safe and beautiful. You bring me light. Hope. Do you know what Anton will do to you if he gets a chance?" He touched the side of her face and she leaned into his touch. "Do you know what would happen to me if you weren't in the world anymore?" he whispered.

She shook her head. "No. What would happen?"

"I'm sliding into a place where I don't feel anymore. Not pain, not fear, not regret. I just live from day to day and kill. That's all I'm becoming. But you make me feel. Anger and frustration, mainly," he said wryly and she raised a brow at him. "But you've awakened something in me that I was beginning to think was dead. Please, don't do this."

A tear fell down Simone's cheek. He touched her so deeply. "I have to do this. Not to prove a point, but because it's what I was born to do. And I'm not going out to find him. No, I have to leave that to you. Stay here while you're out there, and risk losing you." She took his hand and kissed his fingers. "Do you know what would happen to me if *you* weren't in the world anymore?"

He smiled a bit and shook his head. "What?"

"Well, I'd probably get more sleep and my blood pressure would be lower, but you're the other half of me. I can't argue with fate and she sent you to me. You're mine, Kael Gardener. You need some damned manners, but you're good in bed and I kind of like having you around. So I'll make you a deal—I'll do everything I have to do as safely as I can and you do the same."

He sighed deeply. He was drowning in her. He already had allowed himself to care for her more than he should but there was no turning back. He either ended it now or saw it through to the end—whatever that end was.

"Okay. But I'm going to be there when you do this link thing."

"Fine. Just stay out of the way and don't interfere. Believe it or not, we do know how to do this sort of thing. We're strong. As a unit our magic is intense, the connection is our greatest weapon. We're a witches knot. It's in our binding, the melding of empath and dreamer, of reader, young and old and in between. We take witch magic and wizard magic, a touch of Fae and some vampire and we tie it together and create something new. In there, I'm the warrior."

He smiled at her then. At her ferocity and intelligence, and blushed with embarrassment that he'd underestimated her. "I underestimated you. I never, *ever*, thought you were a pretty piece of fluff, but I didn't consider you a fellow warrior and I should have. I'm sorry. And I'm sorry for this afternoon. You're more to me than sex."

She nodded, thrilled that he'd understood her and shown his respect for what she was. "I'll let you make it up to me later."

He laughed and stood up and this time, she took the hand he offered.

* * * * *

When they entered the front parlor where Lee and Alex practiced their magic, everyone looked up nervously and relaxed when they saw that Kael and Simone were holding hands.

"You, sit there with Jagger and Minx. Do not interfere, no matter what. Do not leave this room. Do not, under any circumstances, beak the circle."

"Yes, siren," Kael said with a salute and kissed her lips quickly.

Simone turned to the other Charvez women. "Okay, let's get this show on the road. I don't know what, if anything, I can get from him. Last night I knew he was killing but I didn't stick around long enough to see if I could find out where he was. I think that he won't know how to hold me out. I can keep my defenses up but not all the way. So *Maman, Tante* Marie and *Grand-mère,* I need you to keep the circle tight so he can't see anything but us."

They laid two circles—an inner circle where Em, Lee and Simone would be, and an outer circle where Lou, Marie and Isolde would be. Alex, Con, Aidan and Connor would be outside that, still on the large woven carpet that was itself a protective space.

Once the circles had been drawn, Simone joined hands with her cousins and fell back into herself, surging through the connection she had with the vampire. Em took the information and fed it Lee, who in turn fed it to Aidan through their link.

Water nearby. A pool yes, but more than that, the river. The brackish smell of the Mississippi came through.

There were other vampires. Eight. They were all weaker, younger than Anton. Some under five years changed.

Anton could feel her and he turned inward to face her. "Well hello, pretty. I've got plans for you."

She ignored him, seeking out his deeper thoughts. Where do you go at sunrise? He knew she was there, but as she'd surmised, not how to block her out. He'd underestimated her and for once, Simone was glad of it. He hadn't even imagined that she'd be clever enough to look for his location.

"After I feed, I'll come for you, pretty," he taunted.

Trees. Willows with the branches hanging on the ground. Magnolias in the air. The light was dim, starlight and vampire vision did the work.

Quiet, but for the water and the movement of feet on the ground. She heard as he did. She heard the heartbeat, the very rapid heartbeat of a human, and felt his hunger. The intensity of it staggered her and she lost her grasp.

She came back to herself with a gasp and Lee and Em held her up. "Up. Hold. Him. Out." This came out in short bursts of breath as she felt Anton push back through the link.

She put everything she had into holding him out. Built the walls as high and impenetrable as she could. Thank the heavens for Em and her gift because she was able to translate Simone's magic and take Lee's to push him back. Simone was sure that Anton had just received a very nasty smack on the nose from the Charvez witches.

A few minutes later, after some very agitated questions from Kael and Con as well as Aidan and Alex, they broke the circle. Kael moved forward, pushing others out of the way to grab her, pulling her into his arms.

"Siren, are you all right?"

"I'd say fine, but that's not entirely true. It's not a pleasant thing to be Anton Perdue. He's insane." Even though she'd fed what she saw through Em and into Aidan, they went over it all again. She told them about the scent of the river and the magnolias, of the willows and the other things, like the look of the drive. That there was a human suffering at Anton's hands right at that moment was painful to know.

"That can't be helped. We'll get people out right now. Simone, you did well. You've helped. I'm sorry I underestimated you," Connor said, handing her a tumbler of scotch.

Shrugging, she sipped. "His hunger, I've never felt anything like it. I've been around Aidan when he needed to feed. It's sort of how I feel at ten if I haven't had breakfast. Pangs. But this was awful, like a clawing in his guts."

"The Oathbreakers are ruled by that. They give in and it becomes their sole purpose. Feeding is everything. The Oath protects us from those baser urges and feelings. They repudiate that protection. I'm sorry you had to feel that. I can't imagine how awful it must have been for you." Aidan knelt and pushed the hair from her face.

Kael felt the irrational urge to punch Aidan in the nose for touching Simone with such familiarity.

"I'm glad you don't have to feel it."

Lee squeezed Aidan's shoulder. "Me too."

"Okay, let's get out there. We know enough to know that they're somewhere northwest of here. Probably between here and Baton Rouge. There aren't a lot of houses right on the river that are privately owned, not as lavish as the one Simone saw. In fact, the house looked much more twentieth century than the older smaller ones. That narrows it down too." Connor stood and his men all swept from the room.

"Promise me you'll stay here tonight, Simone. It's so much safer here. Your family is here, you make them stronger and they make you stronger. I'll be worried if you go back home," Kael said softly as he headed toward the door.

"I think I will. My neck hurts a bit and I'm tired. I didn't get much sleep last night," she teased. "Now, you promise me that you'll be safe. You have to come back to me."

He leaned in and brushed his lips over hers quickly. "I'm always safe. I value my life. If I'm not safe, I endanger my people and I'd never do that. And I've got some making up to do. Can I come back here tonight?" He wanted to spend what little time he had left in New Orleans with her.

"Yes. Come back to me, Kael."

He squeezed her hand a final time and was out the door, leaving her heart nervously pounding at his retreating back.

The three cousins stood hand in hand, watching their men drive away toward something very dangerous.

"This is totally stupid, you know," Lee said as they went into the living room.

"You mean the fragile-women stay-at-home thing?" Em said.

"Yes. Okay, I get that I'm not all slayer-type material like Minx is, but I have a lot of magic. More than Alex does. In fact, Alex and I together are really powerful," Lee said, pacing.

"And Con…"

"Con is a warrior and has been for ten thousand years. And it's not magic that's going to catch this vampire, it's physical strength and wiles," Simone interrupted. "Look, I want to go too. But what if we make it worse? Kael and his crew have been doing this for fifteen years. I've never slayed a vampire. Slain? Whatever. The point is, if we go all Lucy and Ethel here we could mess them up. They'll be worried and we can't do any slaying, or slayage or whatever. What if Anton uses us to get to them?"

"But the demon…"

"Simone's right. The battle with the demon was a magical fight. The battles with Angra and Alex's grandfather were magical battles. That's not what the experts seem to think this one is." Em sighed unhappily.

"So we just wait at home? While they're out risking their lives?"

"Would you rather go out there and endanger them?" Simone asked. "I know you're worried. I'm worried. Em is worried. But we can't help them this way. Not right now. That doesn't mean we can't work together in the meantime to strengthen our magic in case they do need it."

Isolde stood up and clapped her hands together twice. "Yes. Good idea, *chère*. Let us work together for a few hours, eh?"

* * * * *

As they drove, Kael methodically loaded the sawed-off with silver shot. His crossbow sat against his back, the silver-tipped arrows in a custom-made quiver at his waist. Twin berettas were strapped to his thighs. His torso and neck were shielded by thin mesh. Lightweight but incredibly effective at repelling vampire bites, it was the same kind of thing researchers used for shark dives only slightly less heavy.

Minx put lipstick on. They called her Minx because she was the pretty bait. She sashayed into the scene and batted her eyelashes and they were on her in record time. Her hair was so black it was blue and it hung straight and smooth as water, gliding over her shoulders and arms. Her full lips were shiny and candy apple red. Vampires had a thing for her pretty cocoa skin and those lush lips. Tonight she was wearing a very short skirt and a tight T-shirt.

Usually before they could get their incisors fully out, she'd delivered a head shot. The prettiest things were often the deadliest. Kael used to be moved by her beauty, attracted by it even as he pushed down any non-brotherly feelings. But he looked at her now and sure, he appreciated how lovely she was, but she failed to move him.

After her lipstick was on, Kael watched as she put her knives in her wrist sheaths and strapped her holster to the small of her back. It would slow her down but she couldn't carry the obvious weaponry that the others did and sustain the illusion. In that way, her job was the most dangerous of all, but she never complained and she did it well.

They followed the twin vans driven by the vampires, the Oathkeepers, as they called themselves. They stopped often and got out, scanning the area. It was hard for Kael but he did feel the difference in the air between the vampires and the ones they called the Oathbreakers. Even that small admission was a difficult one to make to himself. His world was shifting, moving and changing, and he didn't know how to deal with all of it. So for now, he chose not to. To focus on the one sure thing in his life—hunting.

Each time they'd gotten back in the cars and continued driving, Jagger marked the places they checked on a map. From what Kael could tell, the area where Anton could be was shrinking.

At the last stop, they were about an hour and a half away from New Orleans. When they found nothing, Connor came into the RV with Aidan.

"Nothing. I can feel a general disturbance in the area but nothing close enough or specific enough. The problem is that we've been at this for hours and hours and the sun will be coming up and we need to get back."

"We'll come back tomorrow after we've rested. During daylight," Kael said. "We've done this dozens of times, you know."

"I do know and I respect that. But this is my jurisdiction and this Oathbreaker has shamed my people and it's my job to stop him. I..." he looked past Kael and caught sight of Minx and his sentence trailed off.

Minx smiled at him, blushing a bit. Kael saw the interchange and met Jagger's eyes and rolled his own. Amused and annoyed, Kael snapped his fingers a few times. Blinking, Connor came back to attention and turned his attention to Kael.

"That is to say, I'd appreciate it very much if we could do this as a team."

"How many humans need to die so you can get the collar on this?"

Connor blanched and Aidan started to interrupt but Connor put a staying hand on his shoulder.

"You think it's about that?"

"Look, Connor, I appreciate that this is your job and all, but each night we don't catch him means more humans die. Now, I'm not going to say that the lives of humans don't matter to you, but I will say that they matter enough to me to be back here when the sun is highest and he'll be weakest to find this bastard and kill him if I can. This has to end and no, I'm sorry, I'm not going to wait to make the kill with you if we can do it first." Kael did his best to sound diplomatic but he wasn't going to let a vampire and his politics stop him from hunting this sick fuck.

Connor sighed and started to argue but Kael held up his hand. "This isn't negotiable. Cooperating at night is one thing, but that's not going to stop me from hunting when we're most effective and that's during the day when he's weakest."

Connor threw up his hands and left the RV.

"Let's go and get some rest for a few hours and then we'll get back out at one," Kael ordered as they turned the RV around.

"I'm going to drive you back to Simone's, Kael. The rest of us are going to stay at my uncle's place tonight. That way we can have a big 'ol breakfast when we wake up. My uncle is a wicked cook. We'll come get you at one," Cap called back.

"Does everyone know about us or what?" Kael grumbled.

Minx laughed. "It's all over your face. I've never seen you look at anyone the way you look at her. And she looks at you the same way."

"She's not for me, Minx. She's a nice woman to have in my bed for the next few days but she's too soft and pretty. I'd ruin her if I stayed for long."

Minx frowned at him. "You're full of shit. You'll ruin her if you leave. Don't do this, Kael. This woman is more than just a townie you can romance and bed. She's the real thing."

"Exactly. Which is why I'm going to leave her to make room for the guy with the designer duds and the good job in the city. Can you imagine her out in this life? Those pretty fingernails would get chipped. She's not for this life."

"Maybe you're not anymore, either. Have you thought about working with the vampires? Instead of hunting alone, working with them to take the bad guy vamps down?"

The night before, Connor had approached him about joining their crew with his Oathkeepers as a human liaisons and hunters. It would mean steady pay, equipment allowances and backup. Frequently updated intelligence on the Oathbreakers and their movements.

"You think I'm gonna go work for *them*?" He had to admit that he'd thought about it for a good long time. Connor had said that their home base could be in any city. He'd thought about how he and Simone could build a life when he had a regular job.

"You know that they're good people. They have their lawbreakers just like we do. The money is damned good. We could have normal lives. To a point anyway. But we could have houses and we'd go on missions with complete support. We'd hunt like five times a year instead of being on the road all the time. Roots, Kael. Haven't you ever wanted roots?"

"I had roots, Melanie. The vampires came and took them from me," Kael snarled.

"We've all lost loved ones, Kael. But you can make *new* roots. Build something real and stable with Simone," Minx argued.

Jagger watched them both without speaking. Kael knew his friend would have something to say about the whole situation but would wait until he'd mulled it all over first. The man never did or said anything rash.

"We'll talk more about this later. I'll see you at one," Kael tossed out as he grabbed his gym bag and got out of the RV in front of Lee's house. "You know, I feel weird about you all sleeping at your uncle's, Cap. They have a big drive here, why don't you pull in and stay? If you feel weird about bunking inside stay in the RV. You can feel the wards even out here."

"Nah, it's already coming up on dawn. It'll be sunup by the time we get there and we can get a hot breakfast and showers before we bunk down."

"Okay. Well, make it two then. We need all the sleep we can get."

"Gotcha," Cap called out as Kael came down the steps. He caught sight of Simone standing on the porch waiting for him and all of the ugly memories faded. She was his safe harbor and he went toward her, accepting that offer of solace with open arms.

He turned and waved as he jogged up the steps and put his arm around Simone's waist.

"They should stay here," Simone said.

"I asked. I think Cap just wants his aunt's home cooking. They'll be back at two so we should get inside. I've got work to do and the sun is coming up."

Simone waved at the retreating RV and turned to lead Kael into the house. A moment of unease passed through her but she pushed it away, not wanting to mar her time with Kael with bad feelings or an argument.

Chapter Seven

ജ

Kael watched her walk up the grand staircase ahead of him with that sensuous sway to her hips. Her hair was free and swung back and forth as she walked. The scent of her shampoo was in the air, warring with the warm, sexy scent of her skin.

Down a long gallery-style hallway, she opened up a door and motioned him inside. He tossed his bag and looked around. The room was filled with antiques that seemed to fit the house perfectly. It was beautiful, but homey at the same time. In fact, the whole house was that way. It was easy to see the energy that had been put into the furnishings and interiors but at the same time, he never felt uncomfortable sitting on a chair or walking on a rug.

His eyes snagged on the large bed near the French doors leading to what he guessed was the veranda that lined the entire second story of the house.

"Would you like to take a bath? I ran one for you. It should be just cool enough to get into now."

Her voice brought his attention and he looked at her there. So beautiful and sexy. Even in that silky robe and bare feet, face free of makeup and hair down she still looked like a million bucks.

"You ran me a bath? I, uh…yeah, I'd like that." Warmth filled him that she'd gone out of her way to be so thoughtful.

One corner of those sensual lips curved up. She held her hand out and he took it and let himself be led into the bathroom.

A free-standing clawfoot bathtub stood in the center of the room and candles were perched on every surface. The flickering light reflected off the mirrors and walls and gave the room a warm glow.

Simone reached down and trailed her fingers through the water and smiled as she turned back to him. "Perfect. Now, let me help you."

Kael stood, stunned as her gentle hands divested him of his shirt. She walked around him, running her hands over his bare torso and pressing small kisses here and there—over his shoulders and chest, his arms and neck—until she came back to face him again.

Locking eyes with him, she reached out with a single finger and poked him in the chest, pushing him into the chair near the door. *Who had bathrooms with chairs in them?*

All thought regarding the wonder of chairs in bathrooms fled when she dropped to her knees and undid the fastenings on his boots and pulled each off. His socks followed and then she stood up.

He followed and she unbuttoned and unzipped his jeans and pushed them down, along with his underwear. Another devilish smile followed when she saw how hard he was.

She felt the heat radiate from his naked body and delighted in the way his eyes watched her hands as she untied the short robe and let it fall from her body. His pupils widened when he took in her nakedness and he stepped toward her. She stopped him with three fingers against his lips.

"Mmmm mmmm. Bath time first. Then you can make it up to me." She turned and moved to the head of the tub and with a frown he obeyed, slowly stepping into the steamy water.

"Oh god, siren. This feels so good. My muscles are sore." He groaned long and deep when he sat down and slid so that he was up to his neck.

"Good. There's healing oil in the water." She put a hand on his shoulder when he tried to get up. "Oh calm down, you big baby. It will make your muscles feel better. I can't believe that you think I'd do you harm."

"I don't," he protested. "I'm just not used to all of this magic stuff. I know enough defensive magic to repel what some of the older vamps use. But until you, the only magic I encountered was bad magic." He relaxed under the soft kneading of his muscles beneath her fingers. "This, however, is very good magic. You're really excellent at that."

"One of my talents, along with bubbles and toil and troubles," she said dryly.

He laughed even as his eyes slid closed. "Okay, okay. I said I was sorry."

"As a matter of fact, you didn't say you were sorry. But I'll accept your half-assed, arrogant man apology anyway."

Simone looked down at him and smiled. He was such a colossal ass! But so wounded beneath the tough guy veneer. Sweet in his own way. Protective. Courageous. Loyal to his friends. Stubborn. Good in bed. Really good in bed. At first she'd thought he had no sense of humor, but the more she was around him, the more she saw it. It was dark and dry. She liked it. She liked *him*, messed up psyche and all.

"Are you hungry? I have some fruit and cheese here with some good bread. A bit of wine."

He opened his eyes and looked up at her suspiciously. "That's awfully nice of you, siren."

"Why does this surprise you? I'll have you know I'm a very nice person!"

He grabbed her hand and brought it to his lips, kissing her palm. She shivered at the intimate brush of his lips there.

"You're right. You are a nice person. Too nice for the likes of me. But I'll take your fruit and cheese and bread anyway and hold you in my bed as long as I can."

She sighed at how that sounded. Tinged with finality. He still fought their connection. She popped a piece of melon into his mouth and he hummed his satisfaction. "Really good."

"Of course. Here." She fed him a bit of bread with a tiny amount of lemon curd spread over it.

He sat up as he chewed and looked around at her in wonder. "What is that? Oh my god, I'm in lemon heaven!"

She threw her head back and laughed. "That's lemon curd. A friend of the family lives in London and sends it to us. It's good, isn't it?"

"Yes, it's like lemon meringue pie. I love lemon meringue pie. My foster mom used to make it for me on my birthday." For a moment, the look on his face was tender.

She waited silently but he didn't elaborate and she turned back to the platter. She'd taken Em and Lee's advice to heart and she had a plan.

"Here, try this cheese with the apple. Would you like a glass of wine?"

He bit into the tart Granny Smith and the sharp cheddar and moaned in pleasure. "I don't want to get too sleepy just yet." He raised an eyebrow in her direction and she leaned in and kissed him quickly.

"All right. Have some ice water then."

He took several big gulps of the water and handed it back to her. She placed the tray of food on a low table and rolled it up against the side of the tub.

"Eat and I'll get your back."

He hesitated for a moment.

"Let me do this for you. How long has it been since someone pampered you, Kael?"

"I'm used to doing things for myself," he said gruffly, but leaned forward and grabbed more of the juicy melon and popped it into his mouth while she scrubbed his back.

The soft scent of sandalwood filled the room and she rubbed soapy circles across his back and shoulders. At his neck she pressed a kiss to the spot just below his ear. Gooseflesh rose across his skin and she smirked at the back of his head. She was getting to him.

She knew that was the way to get him to let down his walls. To kill him with kindness. And she loved doing it. Kael Gardener needed some pampering, some love. It was clear in how he related to the world, that he wasn't used to the luxury of having love heaped on him. She'd never actually given anyone a bath before but this was nice. Taking care of him felt good and heaven knew he needed some TLC. Simone had grown up with a loving family, with caresses and kisses and hugs, and there wasn't a day that went by when at least three people hadn't told her they loved her. She wanted to be that for him, show him there was another way to live.

Before long he was relaxed enough that he didn't complain when she washed from the tips of his fingers up to his underarms on both sides. He looked up at her as she moved the table out of the way and sat on the edge of the tub.

Tenderly, she washed his feet and his calves and her hands were under the water as she brushed up his thighs and over his extremely hard cock.

He watched her, drank her in as she ministered to him. He'd never felt taken care of before. Not like this. He could feel how much she cared about him in the way she held his hand and moved the washcloth across his body. The food was thoughtful and he was always hungry when he came back from a night out hunting.

He allowed himself to imagine this every night, or at least on a regular basis. Coming home to Simone waiting at the door for him. His woman, his life, his house. He'd never permitted himself to want those things before and truthfully, he'd never missed the wanting. Until now. Until her.

He held her hands back and dunked himself under the water. When he emerged, standing up, water sluiced down his muscles. Simone's greedy gaze followed the beads of moisture until she got to his cock and stopped with a visible gulp.

"I seem to have a problem, siren," he said in a growl.

"Oh?" Simone replied faintly as she took him in.

He grinned at her like a predator and she blushed. He liked that. Taking the towel out of her hands, he stepped out, dried himself quickly and tossed it on the rack.

"Oh yes. You see, I'm in pain and only you can make it better."

She laughed then—a sultry, honeyed sound. "Is that so?" Her head was cocked and her hair was a silky drape over one breast. The other was bare to his gaze, inviting his hands. His lips.

"Doctor, I seem to have this swelling that won't go down." He led her to the bed and she climbed up and turned to face him, on her knees.

"Hmm. Maybe if I go down, the swelling will."

"I think that's a sound plan worth a try," he said with a grin as she reached out and pulled him to the bed with her.

His laughter died when she scrambled atop him and looked down into his face with those big golden eyes.

Her hair was a curtain around their faces when she leaned down to take his lips. There was nothing but the two of them. No one. No Oathbreakers, no vampires, no Faeries, no troubled childhood. Just Kael and Simone and their lips sliding together.

Oh how she loved his taste! She loved to be above him, the power of the pace in her hands, in her control. She took long luscious draws on his lips, loving the way the hairs of his goatee tickled her chin. He tasted of melon and a hint of lemon and that essential Kael that was imprinted in her very soul.

She moved from his lips and across his cheekbone, soft kisses over his eyelid and brow bone. She poured everything she felt for him into those kisses, her hand softly kneading his shoulders as she did.

"Simone," Kael murmured softly, his hands sliding up her thighs and around to cup her ass.

"Mmmm?" she hummed into his ear and followed up with a lick around the shell of his ear, over those damnable sexy earrings. She couldn't believe she actually thought a man with tattoos and earrings was sexy. But oh, he was.

"Please."

She kissed down his neck and over the hollow of his throat where his pulse beat madly. Her tongue swirled in that warm dent and he gave a shuddering breath, hands tightening on her ass.

Taking her time, she kissed across his collarbone and over the hard muscle of his pecs.

"Simone!"

She stopped and looked up at him with a catlike smile. "Kael, patience is well rewarded."

"I don't want to be patient! I want you to suck my cock. Come on, please, siren. I want you so badly."

"Kael, darlin', some things can't be rushed. Now hush up or I'll stop." She bent again and tugged each nipple ring in her teeth, alternating between them. He arched up off the bed with a groan of pleasure.

Her lips skimmed over the hard planes of his abdomen and she licked and then nibbled on his bellybutton and then across that supersensitive skin between navel and groin. He'd let go of her bottom and was now running his fingers through her hair.

She scooted down so that she was between his thighs and looked up at him wearing that smile. She never broke eye contact as she darted her tongue out and drew it slowly up the throbbing length of his cock, but she did allow herself to close her eyes for a brief moment when she drew her tongue over the bead of semen that had gathered at the eye.

"Oh dear god. Simone, you're going to kill me," he groaned as his hands tightened in her hair.

"Mmmmm," she hummed in satisfaction as her mouth enveloped him and she pulled him into her body. Under her tongue veins were alive, he was hard and hot and very sensitive. He nearly jumped off the bed when she dug the tip of her tongue into that sweet spot just beneath the head of his cock and flicked it.

She stopped for a moment. "You know, I read once, probably in Cosmo, that this spot," she rubbed her thumb in that slick place she'd just licked, "was similar to a woman's clit."

"Simone," Kael said through clenched teeth. "Can we have the biology lesson later?"

She laughed and took him back in her mouth, this time as deeply as she could. Her fingers pressed against that place just behind his balls and he groaned raggedly. Her pace was slow and sure. She kept him nice and wet as she licked and sucked and even nibbled a bit.

She could feel him get harder and harder. The surface of the skin of his cock felt nearly electric with the gathering energy of his orgasm. She loved that she made him feel that way, loved that he desired her so much.

"Oh god, I'm so close." His words were a taut whisper. His hands held her head gently and he rolled his hips up to meet her mouth. His thigh muscles tightened and he cried low and hoarse as he began to come in wave after wave.

His essence flooded her as his taste filled her. Her ears devoured the sound of his pleasure, of the sound of her name on his lips.

At long last he relaxed and she pulled back with a small kiss to the head of his cock.

She snuggled up next to his body and he sighed in contentment. "You're a terrible tease, you know that, siren?"

"I am most certainly not a tease! A tease never delivers. I delivered, I just did it on my own schedule. It was worth it, wasn't it?" The drawl of her voice was lazy and smoky, teasing. It was another thing that he loved about her. He sighed inwardly. Yeah, loved. He shoved it away and turned his thoughts back to the present.

He grinned. "That it was, Simone. Now, once I get feeling back in my legs, it's going to be your turn."

"Oh good. I'll be waiting eagerly for that."

He laughed and she loved the sound. A real laugh. Not a chuckle or a quick bit of amusement but something filled with joy. The laugh was a bit rusty, like he didn't do it very often and his body didn't quite remember how. Her heart ached for him and once again she vowed to show him how love could revolutionize his life.

She was still planning when she found herself on her back with him looming over her. "Turnabout is fair play, siren."

"Oh yes, please!"

He laughed again and then took her lips. Her kisses to him had been sweet and delicious. His kiss that moment was devastating in its carnality. His tongue didn't slide into her mouth, it seduced her and then shattered her into tiny pieces. His teeth nipped her bottom lip.

He took tiny bites across her jawline and then down her neck.

When he got to her breasts he pushed them together so that he could flick the nipples with his tongue over and over again. He was relentless. Licking and sucking and the dragging the edge of his teeth over her nipples until she was writhing beneath him, making sounds of inarticulate entreaty.

Just before she was sure she'd die, he moved down her body and pushed her thighs open wide.

"Oh, siren. You're so wet and pink for me. Your pussy is so beautiful." To underline that he leaned in to give her a lick and she shuddered as the endorphins slid through her body.

His tongue speared into her and curled upward, gathering her honey, stroking the inside of her pussy.

She was really wet. She felt the heat of her cream on her thighs, sliding down her pussy. He moved up to suckle her clit and pushed two fingers into her, replacing his tongue.

"Oh! Yes," she moaned. "More, oh please more."

He gathered her moisture with the fingertips of his free hand and then tickled the star of her rear passage with them. She made a flat sound and stiffened.

"Siren, relax and trust me to make you feel good," he said, lips against her labia.

She took a deep breath and let go, trusting him to do that very thing. He slowly sucked her clit in and out of his mouth as he fucked her with his fingers. Her entire body was beginning to tremble as pleasure began to build up against the inevitable storm of orgasm. It was in her mouth, tingling her scalp and fingertips.

She could feel it begin to settle into her body the way that you know a really powerful orgasm is coming. She kept thinking it would come but it stayed just out of reach until he slid his thumb into her rear passage, and it exploded around her.

Orgasm, quicksilver, ran through her, drowning her, submerging her in the intensity of feeling that only happened very rarely. Her body bowed up off the mattress, pussy pressed to his mouth.

Burst after burst of pleasure rolled through her as a long, guttural growl issued from her gut. It was as if he was pulling something primal from deep inside of her body.

His pace slowed and he finally pulled back to press a kiss to her lower stomach. Looking into her face, he was laid bare. Defenseless against what he saw there, what he felt in her touch, heard in her voice, tasted on his lips. Yep, he loved her. Loved her so much he was utterly terrified by it.

"I love you, Kael."

He closed his eyes for a moment, humbled by the gift of love from this woman. It awed him, it comforted him, it thrilled him and it frightened him.

"Don't, Simone. I have nothing to give to you. Don't expect anything from me but today and let's just have that." The sadness in his voice was so sharp and deep that Simone actually felt her gut cramp at the sound of it.

"Oh, Kael. Love isn't tit for tat. I don't love you only if you love me too. I don't love you because it's easy or because I expect anything in return. Real love doesn't expect favors."

She reached up and touched his face and he was unable to resist turning into her touch and kissing her palm.

"I want to make love to you," he murmured.

She quirked up a corner of her mouth. "By all means."

He nudged her thighs open and knelt between them. He looked panicked for a moment and she sighed. Reaching back, she pulled a condom out from under the pillow behind her and handed it to him. "You know, it's your responsibility to provide birth control too."

He nodded solemnly. "You're right. I will go and buy a big box tomorrow. Or later today anyway." A quick rip and roll and he was sheathed and ready to go, bending over her body, pushing his cock into her slick heat.

She groaned as he entered her body, filling her, sating her. "Are you only being agreeable because you want to get laid?"

He barked out a laugh. "I didn't think that would work on you."

He hilted and they both stilled, enjoying the moment.

"Oh, good answer, Sparky."

She was slick from her orgasm and his way was eased by her honey. Still, each slow thrust he made into her body was received by a pussy so tight and so very hot that he thought he'd lose his mind. Her body was made for his, he couldn't deny it. He wanted to, but he couldn't. That didn't change the basic fact that he had nothing to offer this woman beyond the short time he'd be in New Orleans and he couldn't afford to let her, or himself, hope for more.

His heart ached at that thought and instead he relished each embrace of her flesh around his. He devoured the memory of her face, the curve of her lips, the way the pulse beat so strongly at the hollow of her throat. He committed her voice to memory and the feel of her skin to his heart. Because he knew without a moment's doubt that there would be no one else for him. Ever.

Simone looked into his eyes and he saw the hurt there. She gave a soft, sad smile and shook her head. "Stop planning to leave me, Kael. Just live. Here with me now. We can deal with the rest later."

He touched his forehead to hers and nodded.

The love they made was slow and achingly tender and when it was over he pulled her close, into the shelter of his body, and tried to sleep. It would be ending soon and no matter what happened, he'd be leaving New Orleans without her.

* * * * *

After he'd tossed and turned for an hour and finally found sleep just before seven-thirty, Simone got out of bed with a kiss to his forehead.

She took a shower and went downstairs and saw Em sitting at the breakfast table with some tea and the morning paper.

Em looked up at Simone and gave her a sad smile. "How was it?"

Simone sighed, poured herself a cup of coffee and sat down. "I'm going to lose him. No. I don't suppose I've ever had him. I can't get through to him. I'm not worth it to him to give up his life on the road and build something with." Tears stung her eyes.

Em reached out and squeezed her hand. "*Bébé,* he loves you. He does. He knows you're his. This will work out. It has to. It was meant to. We did not survive the demon lord and Angra and Katrina and Rita for you to be so heartbroken. We survived...*you* survived for a reason. Kael Gardener is that reason. You are meant for him. You are meant to save him."

Lee wandered into the room and hugged Simone from behind. "You are special, Simone. You are on this Earth for a reason. I know it seems dark right now, but things will out the way they're supposed to. You exist to serve a higher purpose."

Simone put her head down on the table and wept while her cousins held her and whispered all the right things.

After she'd cried herself out, the three witches worked on their magic together with Alex, who tried not to be seen frowning at the forlorn look on Simone's face.

* * * * *

The women were making lunch and Alex was working in the office. Max and the other humans who worked with the Oathkeepers were stationed around the house and checking in on a regular basis. Soon Simone would go up and wake Kael to get ready to meet his crew.

Simone was drying her hands after tossing the salad when she spun and turned to Em, who'd gone white-faced.

The terror that ran through her nearly sent her to her knees. Pain, fear, rage. Something had happened to Kael's crew. Her friendship with Minx had created a strong link between them. And now Minx was in big trouble. So much emotion roiled through her, her hands trembled and her stomach threatened to riot.

"No!" Simone gasped and took off upstairs at a run. "Kael!" she screamed as she ran, ignoring the people coming out of the rooms of the house, ready for a battle.

She burst into the bedroom as he was pulling on his jeans, looking panicked. "What? What is it, siren?"

"It's your crew. I think something is wrong. Oh god."

He pushed past her to his phone, flipped it open and punched the numbers.

Em and Con came into the room with Lee and Alex in time to catch Kael's curse as he tried another number. And another.

He turned back to Simone and grabbed her. "What the fuck is going on? Where are they?"

"I don't know. I just felt that something happened. Minx, Minx and I have become friends, I felt…"

"What do you mean you don't know? I thought you were a witch! What use are these powers of yours, then? Why didn't you tell me earlier?" he screamed in her face.

And felt himself thrown against the wall. When the stars cleared he saw Con above him with a snarl on his lips. "What did I tell you about that?"

"These are my people! The closest thing I have to a family. I should have protected them. Being with you took my concentration off them and look what happened!" he yelled at Simone.

Simone was shaking with emotion. "I will help you find them. Get dressed. I'll be downstairs waiting." She walked out of the room without looking at him.

"Gods, man! What is wrong with you? Salvation is right there in her arms and you push her away over and over. Don't you think you've hurt her enough?" Alex asked Kael as he pulled a shirt on and grabbed his bag.

"I'm damnation to everyone I touch, Alex." Kael turned and walked past Lee, who had to clench her fists to keep from punching him.

Simone was waiting at the front door, looking out the windows. Without looking up at his approach, she nodded to Max and Con. "Let's go."

Kael grabbed her arm. "Siren, you aren't going anywhere."

She pulled herself out of his grasp. "Don't. Don't touch me and don't call me anything but my given name. I will go where I want when I want. You have no say in *anything* to do with my life. If you want to find your friends, you need me and my resources. As such, I will say where I go and when. If these terms are unacceptable to you, the door is just there. But remember that your pride won't save your people."

He flinched at the ice in her eyes. "I don't want you to get hurt." He started to reach out to touch her again but she took a step back.

She focused on him then. "Too late. Now get your things. Max is going to take us in one of their vans. Con is coming along with Alex, Lee and Em."

He stood there a moment, weighing his options, but she was right. She held the cards. With an explosive breath, he stormed outside and they followed.

"Are you going to be all right?" Em murmured.

"I am going to kill the next person who asks me that. Just sayin'." Simone climbed into the back of the van, avoiding the front, where Max and Kael were sitting.

"Head toward Cap's uncle's house. I'm going to use the link," Simone called out as they pulled out of the driveway.

"Damn it, s-Simone," Kael snarled, stopping himself from using his nickname for her. "This is too dangerous for you."

"I will find them. You will get them back and stop Anton Perdue and you will leave just like you planned. Nice and tidy. In order for us to find them, we have to find Anton. In order for that to happen we have to use the one big weapon we have. That's my link with him."

He wanted to touch her, to haul her into his arms and apologize for hurting her earlier. Wanted to assure her he'd never leave her because he loved her and she was his fucking soul. But he couldn't. How could he live in a world without her? And he lived a dangerous life, he knew his job could bring her harm and he couldn't live without knowing she was somewhere living her life, safe. Couldn't live with himself if he brought this life of his into hers, tainting that beautiful existence with blood and terror and sharp white teeth. No, it was better this way. Make a clean break once he got his people back. It was all he had to keep him from running away with her at that very moment.

"Fine. But damn you, be careful."

Her eyes flashed something tender for a moment and then it was gone.

The drive to Metairie was tense and quiet. Lee looked over at Em and Con and she knew they were more concerned with Simone's wellbeing than anything else. Yes, they cared about the members of Kael's crew, but Simone was theirs and she was in so much pain that even Lee could feel it.

On top of all of that, Aidan and Connor were going to be hot when they woke up. Lee knew how angry they'd be, but she also knew that she and Em were necessary to link up with Simone to protect her when she used her connection with the Oathbreaker. Alex's magic would be a big help and Con wasn't the most feared Faerie warrior in thousands of years for nothing.

It wasn't optimal, but it had to be enough.

* * * * *

Simone watched the back of Kael's head as they drove. She felt Em's anxiety for her wellbeing, Con's worry over all of them, Max's concern for Connor and the other vampires and his anger at Kael's mistreatment of Simone.

She looked over and caught Alex's eye and he winked at her. Of all the people there, Alex probably understood the best. He had been so achingly lonely when he'd come to New Orleans two years before. Lee and Aidan had filled him up and they'd all three embraced that.

She just didn't know what to do. She was a goal-oriented person, had always been successful at whatever she put her mind to, and now she didn't know if that would make any difference.

Sure, Simone believed Em when Em told her that Kael loved her. She saw it herself when he allowed her in, even just a little bit. She certainly loved him. But there was no way she could live with a man who struck out rather than let anyone get close. It was one thing to woo him, to show him how much she loved him. It was another to let him hurt her over and over. She couldn't...wouldn't live that way.

She did love him. So much her heart ached with her desire to go to him and comfort him. But she knew he wouldn't accept it and she couldn't bear another rebuff from him right then.

But she was pulled from her thoughts as they approached the house.

"Oh god!" Em hunched over and Simone was out the door before they'd come to a stop.

Alex grabbed her and she shook him off. "Let me go! There's no one here. The threat is gone but the energy is still here!"

"Damn it, Simone, get back in the van. You don't know what's waiting inside." Kael looked at the broken-down front door and his sawed-off was in his hands, the weight familiar and comforting.

She turned to him. "I do know. I can feel it. I can feel what they all felt," she ended on a gag and he moved to her side quickly but she shook her head and took a deep breath. "There's no one here now. No one alive, anyway."

Con reached out and stepped in front of Kael. "Let me check for booby traps."

Kael stopped, nodded once and waited for Con, who went up onto the porch, cocking his head. The air rippled and he was gone and then back moments later.

"It's clear. There are bodies inside. Two elderly humans. Shot in the head after they'd been tortured. No signs of anyone else."

Simone closed her eyes and Em approached and took her hand.

"Simone, please, just be careful," Kael said quietly and she smiled sadly and nodded.

"Are you sure you want to do this, *mo fiach*?" Con asked his wife.

Em smiled at his nickname for her and nodded. "It has to be done."

They walked into the house with Max and Con.

The stench of death and pain hung in the air, thick and cloying. The screams, silenced now in death, still reverberated in psychic echo. Simone knew that it would be that way for a very long time to come. This kind of horror didn't dissipate easily or quickly.

She tried to wall all of that out and focus on the different types of energies still in the air like a stain. Minx's life energy was there, not extinguished, as it left the house. Cap's, Jagger's and Daniel's too. All alive at the time they were taken from the house. Other unknown humans with that sick smear of Anton on them.

Em turned and they compared what they felt quietly with Con and Max at the ready.

* * * * *

After the others had gone inside, Kael turned to Lee. "What is going on?" Kael demanded. Lee narrowed her eyes at him and poked him hard in the chest.

"Look here, my cousin may be in love with you but I'm not. If you don't shut your mouth and start treating her with the respect and dignity she deserves I swear to you that I'll go into the bayou and curse your ass! I know people, Kael Gardener."

He looked down into her face and flinched at how livid she was.

"She doesn't love me. She doesn't need me." But oh what a liar he was. He hated that. He'd never lied other than to get out of a tight spot before. Certainly never about someone he cared about.

"Man oh man! You are the most arrogant idiot I've ever met. Of course she loves you! You're her man and you know it. And I wish she didn't need you. But she does. She'll never find true happiness with anyone else. You are hers. What I don't understand is why you're going to fuck that up."

"She doesn't need me in her life, Lee. She needs someone nice with a good job. I can only bring her pain. There are other men, other loves. She'll move on once I'm gone."

"And what about you? Are you so self-destructive that you'll just give up the one thing that can save your soul? Because the flip side of you being hers is that she's yours. There'll never be anyone else for you. Do you think that pushing away everything important will save her? Would you give her a life of unhappiness in some misguided attempt to be a bigger person? Because she needs you, Kael. You need her. You two are meant for each other and if you just accept that things will work out the way they're supposed to."

Before he could answer, the others came out of the house and into the yard.

"There were several humans. Stained by the Oathbreakers. There was terror. So much terror. Fury. Your crew were all still alive when they left here," Simone said, looking into his face. There was a slight tremor in her voice but she held herself together well.

"I need to try and link with Anton. He'll be at rest but I think I may be able to manipulate him when he's sleeping. Aidan told me that Oathbreakers are more tied to the sun than the rest of vampires. He won't have the strength to fight me off."

Kael looked at her, into the face of this woman he loved so much, and his heart constricted in his chest in fear for her. In fear for his crew.

"I don't like it, but if we don't get to them before Anton wakes up they're as good as dead. Let me go through the house to see if they've left any clues for me. Don't start until I get back."

He threw her a hard look and went up the steps and onto the porch. He knelt and examined the doorway and the marks on the railing. They'd worked out some signals to leave in case of kidnapping. Charity had left them, but the vampires had wanted to be found and they'd left plenty of their own. In the end, it hadn't saved Charity.

There was a bootmark low on the wall just inside the house. Jagger's boot. Pain sliced through Kael at the thought of losing his best friend and the brother of his heart. Of failing them. At least Jagger had shoes on. At least they hadn't been pulled out of bed.

He tried to be dispassionate as he looked at the battered bodies of Cap's aunt and uncle. At least they weren't turned or had had their throats ripped out. Kael had seen enough misery in his life to always try and look for something positive in the situation. Death didn't look exceptionally long in coming for them. The bodies were just cool so the trail would still be warm. That meant the human servants had stormed the house an hour before, more or less.

He looked carefully around and saw that Minx had dropped her watch. He picked it up with a quiet exclamation and looked at the time on the face. "Good girl, Minx." She'd stopped it at 12:41. He looked at his own watch, it was two o'clock. A little over an hour. Hope burst through him, and he also realized that if Simone hadn't felt whatever it was she felt and run to him that he wouldn't have realized there was a problem until far later. He probably would have been with them when they were taken. If their lives were saved, it would be due to her.

Sighing, he made a careful pass through the house, went back outside and saw that they'd moved to the van and had turned on the air conditioning. Kael saw that the RV was still parked next to the house and motioned them all over.

He looked carefully, but saw no signs of tampering and went inside. Simone came in, the others followed. Max would follow them in the van.

"I found a sign, Minx's watch that she'd stopped at the time I believe they left the house. It was just over an hour ago." As he spoke he powered everything up and pulled out weapons, laying them on the table.

"Okay. I'm going to try to use the link. Em and Lee are going to help me and Alex and Con will watch over them. Don't interrupt. Let one of them stop it. If they don't stop it, assume it doesn't need to be stopped." Simone opened up her bag, pulled out a pouch of sand and drew two concentric circles, one that she was in with Em and Lee and one outside that, where Con and Alex stood.

The Charvez witches sat and linked hands. The magic that spilled through the space was like a warm tide and it prickled the hairs on the back of Kael's neck.

Con looked up at him. "Drive east."

Kael nodded and jumped into the driver's seat and they drove away from the house. They'd have to deal with the cops later. Con had laid a spell on the place so that no one would notice anything amiss until they were ready.

Simone's eyes were closed as she let down the walls that held out her link with Anton Perdue. It was murky and quiet. That didn't, however, mean that it was easy. No, even at rest, Anton's mind and energy were a crazy maze of rage and evil.

His defenses were lax though, and she was able to push her way in and see into his mind. She just had to figure it out once she got there. She handed back what she could to Em, who was sending it to Con.

She saw his memories, where he ordered his humans to stake out the house in New Orleans and the comings and goings of the RV. Saw the moment when they'd reported they'd found Cap's aunt and uncle's house and Anton's orders to take them when they could do it, when they'd be weakest.

She saw the long halls of the house they were in. Saw the outdoor area where they showered after they'd killed. Best of all, she saw the ride back to the mansion after they'd hunted.

She got all she could and pulled away, erecting those walls high and thick on her way out. She didn't want him back in her head again. She'd seen his plans for her and hoped that Kael would keep his promise if it came to that.

When she opened her eyes Em was glaring at her. "You will not! He will not do any such thing!"

Simone knew what her cousin was talking about. She shook her head and touched Em's cheek. "Yes. It has to be done. You know what would happen if he turned me." She looked up at Con and Alex. "They know."

"It won't come to that and we will not discuss it further," Con said tersely. "May we break the circle?"

Em sighed and nodded and they broke the circle.

"Alex or Con, can you drive? I need to prepare the weapons."

Alex nodded and went up to take over for Kael, who then set about loading the various weapons and strapping them on.

Simone picked up a Glock. "Do you have a rig for this?"

He looked at her and raised a brow. "Not for you I don't."

"What does that mean?"

He looked at her, hair up in a ponytail, in denim shorts and tennis shoes and a T- shirt. Even casual she looked magnificent—and utterly incompatible with shooting and fighting vampires.

"Si-Simone, this is going to get ugly. You will stay out here in the RV in case we need to call for backup."

"Bull! In the first place, my father was a sports shooter. Yes, I don't suppose you thought we came with male relatives other than husbands. But he was a champion shot in his youth and taught me and my brothers. They have a decent aptitude at it. I, on the other hand, am a very good shot. Can't say that I know much about sawed-off shotguns, but I know how to use a double barrel shotgun, and I've shot most handguns, all the ones I see here. You need all the help you can get. Lee will stay back here. Em has the ability to shimmer in and out of space-time and Con is a warrior, you'll need his strength and both their magic. Alex is a powerful wizard, you'll need him too."

"I am so not staying here!" Lee exclaimed.

"Yes you are!" Alex yelled back. "She's right. Someone needs to stay and keep the folks back at the house informed so they can all get here as soon as it's dark."

"We'd better hope like hell that we get this taken care of before dark." Kael's face was grim as he tried to strap on his gear with hands shaking in fear and frustration over Simone's presence. He went into every hunt worried about his people but this was different and he didn't like feeling so damned vulnerable.

Simone sighed and slapped his hands away as she fastened the vest for him and tightened the harness for the crossbow.

"You all have to wear vests." Kael squeezed Simone's hand in thanks.

Con and Em were instantly outfitted with them and Simone couldn't help but laugh at Kael's surprise.

She tossed a vest to Alex, and Con helped him while she questioned her sanity as Kael strapped hers on. His proximity was maddening. There was so much to say and it wasn't the right time. But if something happened…

He stood in front of her. "Where do you carry?"

"Let's use the thigh holsters. I'm not exceptional with knife throwing but I can stab and filet with the best of them. My daddy was a hunter too."

Kael looked as though he was going to argue with her, but clenched his teeth with an audible click. He pulled out a knife with a long blade and a sheath. He wove a belt through the loops on her shorts and hooked the sheath through the belt,

"I swear to you, siren, that if you get hurt or take unnecessary risks I will kick your pretty ass. Stay behind me. You'll just be dealing with humans, but humans can shoot guns." He hesitated and looked as if he was going to say something else, but shook his head and Simone sighed.

"We're about three miles out from the mansion, Kael. This thing is as conspicuous as they come. Let's park in that wooded spot just up there and walk in," Con said quietly and Kael nodded.

Alex pulled the RV as far off the road as he could and put on his vest as they all looked at each other. Max came into the RV some moments later.

"No one said I'd be waiting in the car three miles away!" Lee protested.

Kael handed each one of them an earpiece with a highly sensitive mic. He held the last one out to Lee. "We'll all be connected via this comm link. You'll hear the whole thing. You said you took out a demon so I'm trusting you to know when to call for backup. Remember that cops may very easily get killed in there, so mind who you call."

"Okay." Lee put the earphone in and adjusted it. Each of the rest adjusted theirs and did a test to be sure everything worked.

"These have just under a four mile range so Lee should be able to continue to hear us just fine." Kael pulled out a map of the area and together with Con figured out where they were. Only about a mile from where they'd stopped the night before. *Damn it,* they should have continued the search instead of going back!

"Em and I will take Kael and Max first and then come back for Alex and Simone." He pointed to a place on the map. "I think this looks best. The river vegetation should still be thick enough here that no one will expect us to come at the house from that direction."

Kael nodded. "Good idea. Now, the house will be big. Anton is known for living in great luxury and he will be sleeping in a regular bedroom, like Aidan does. My guess is that the room that Anton sleeps in will be heavily guarded. The human servants usually sleep on a different floor or a different wing of the house and usually in shifts to have nighttime servants and ones who are up in the daytime. They're probably holding my crew away from where Anton sleeps so as not to disturb his rest with the blood and excitable humans."

Max checked over the weapons and vest he was wearing and nodded. Kael did the same and Em and Con touched them both and were gone.

"Alex, please be careful. If something happens to any of you, I don't know what I'd do."

Alex looked at Lee and smiled softly, kissing her quickly. "Of course. We're going to be fine." He turned back to Simone. "And when we get back and all this is over, we're going to fix this thing between you and Kael."

Before Simone could answer, Em and Con shimmered back into the RV and took them to the spot where the others were waiting.

Kael was looking through binoculars at the house just above the banks. "There's enough cover to get us to the side of the house. Looks like French doors leading from that veranda there. From what I can see it's a library of some kind. Let's go in there and see what we can find. Stay low and be quiet. Keep behind me and Con. Max will take the rear." The last was pointed at Simone, who rolled her eyes but nodded.

As silently as they could, they approached the house, Em and Simone walking with Max just behind them. Simone could feel the humans in the house and relief rushed through her when she felt Minx. Not fear, calculation. Simone let out a soft breath. Her new friend wasn't terrified, she was planning.

She tapped the mic like Kael had told them to and he stopped and crouched. "I can feel Minx. She's alive and planning," Simone said, her voice barely audible.

Kael closed his eyes for a moment and relief passed over his face. He nodded and they continued up to the house. Con shimmered inside, checked for wires or an alarm, and finding none, opened the doors to let everyone in.

"Con, you stick with Em and Simone. Alex, you're with me and Max. Stick close together and shoot it if it threatens you in any way. Silver shot will kill vampires, but a good head shot will kill humans or vampires."

"No. Look, Em can shimmer me out if necessary but Con can do that too. They should be split up because of that," Simone argued. Con's face looked pained at being separated from Em but he nodded.

"I'll come with you and…"

Kael's hand came up to cut her off. "I am in charge here. A mission like this isn't a democracy, siren. You have a good point. You and Con with me. Alex, Max and Em together."

Simone bit off her retort and instead inclined her head in agreement.

"Max, stick close to this room and keep an eye out. If it goes bad, Em you get Alex the hell out of here and Con will take Simone. Max and I have dealt with this before, we can get out on our own."

They crossed to the door and opened it quietly, looking out. Once they were sure no one was in the hallway they walked out. Simone put a hand on Kael's arm as she closed her eyes. She kept her link with Anton closed but opened herself to the emotions of others in the house.

After a few long moments she opened her eyes and said quietly into the mic, "Minx. I can feel her. Most of the emotions in the house are coming from the West."

"That's where we'll go, then."

"Let's all just go. We're stronger that way," Max said. Kael sighed but agreed and they headed out toward the landing. They'd come in at the side of the house where it was level with the ground, but in truth they were on the second floor.

There were quiet sounds coming from below and they slowly ascended. Simone pointed down a long hallway and that's the way they went. Before the bend in the hall, Kael put his hand up to stop them.

He and Max slowly crept up and crouched just before the turn. Kael pulled out a small gadget with a mirror on the end of it and bent it around the corner and the two came back.

"There are three men guarding a door at the end of the hallway. Con, how are you with a handgun?"

Con gave Kael an arrogant sneer and Kael grinned. "Good. I'm guessing you don't need one."

Con looked down and there were weapons strapped to his thighs.

"Let's go then. Keep it quiet and quick. We don't know how many others are here in the house or what's behind that door."

"We've got your back," Alex said.

Simone watched in awe as Kael turned into a hunter. No, he turned into something deadly. His eyes went flat and he walked around that corner almost casually and fired two shots. Max and Con did the same. Their weapons all had silencers, so it was a lot quieter than Simone thought it would be in that hallway.

Quickly then, they moved and shifted the bodies out of the way.

Simone stood outside the doors with Em and they closed their eyes.

"Five humans. I can pick up Minx and Jagger. I don't know who else is in there."

"Max, you go high, I'll go low. Con, head on in straight. Simone, you shoot anyone trying to escape this room, you got me?"

Simone nodded.

"Em, get her out of here if it gets bad. I'm putting her life in your hands."

Em gave him the thumbs up and Alex turned his back to cover the rear should anyone come from that direction.

Simone put her back to one wall and Em stood against the other. Both had weapons out.

Con kicked the doors open and they stormed into the room. Simone said a silent prayer that they'd all be okay.

Kael went low and the first thing he saw was a man spinning and grabbing a weapon. He sighted down his arm, squeezed the trigger three times and the man fell. He saw Jagger lying on a bed, arms chained but conscious, a gag in his mouth.

Con shot a man to Kael's left and Max went farther into the room and gave the all clear sign.

Cap was in a chair, but beaten pretty severely. Minx was in another chair and Con was untying her. Daniel was nowhere to be found.

"Where is Daniel?" Kael asked Jagger as he untied him.

"I don't know. Cap…he's pretty bad."

Em looked at him. Simone at the door, her back to them, still eyed the corridor with Alex. Kael looked at Max, who nodded sharply and went out to stand guard with Alex.

"Em, take him back to the RV. Lee, Em is coming with Cap. He's bad off," Kael said into the headset and the two shimmered out of the room.

"She'll take you next," he said to Jagger.

"I don't think so. I'm fine. Let's get Daniel, kill us a vamp or five and get the fuck out of here." Jagger stood up and massaged his wrists.

Kael looked him up and down, shrugged and handed him a weapon. Em came back and started to take Minx back.

"No! I'm staying to find Daniel."

"Minx, I can see your arm is broken. Em has strong healing magic, go on back and take care of Cap. I'm staying here until this is over," Con said and Em looked at him. She saw the resolve on his face. Con was a warrior. He believed in a code of conduct, of courage and doing what was right.

"Yes. Em can take Minx back to help Cap and we'll get back as soon as we find Daniel," Simone said.

"You're not going anywhere but back to that RV." Kael's face was hard.

"Shut up. You need my weapon and you need my gift."

Em shimmered out with Minx, making the decision, and Kael grimaced.

"Fine. Jagger, did you see anyone else? How many servants are here? Why did they take Daniel?"

"I don't know. Probably just to fuck with us. There were three more who left with Daniel."

Simone opened herself up again. "The only other feelings I'm getting are faint. Humans, in that direction." She pointed back the way they'd come.

Kael and Max took point, Con and Jagger flanked around Alex and Simone. They crept through the house and a wave of terror washed through Simone and she gasped. They spun to see her and Kael was at her side.

"What is it?"

"Let's keep moving, they're just up here. It's bad…"

There was another set of hallways, but at the end the doors of this room were open and the stench of burning flesh gagged Simone.

Jagger and Kael stormed the room and the muffled sounds of shots were heard, followed by the thud of falling bodies.

"Jaysus," Con breathed as they got to where Daniel was chained to a wall. He bore cigarette burns all over his chest and arms. Con untied him quickly and was gone.

"Fucking bastards. Let's find these vampires and kill them now, while they're weak. I want this done." Jagger's mouth was tight.

"Con will be gone for a while. Em will be tired from healing Minx and Cap, and Daniel looked like they'd done a lot more to him than the burns," Simone said quietly.

"Then you and Alex go out the way we came in. Take the path next to the river and head west after half a mile or so and you'll get back to the road. It won't be too far to the RV. I won't have you see what's going to happen. You've seen enough."

Simone began to argue but Alex took her by the arm. "They're right, Minnie. They don't need you now. All the humans are dead. Let's go. You aren't meant for this."

Simone looked back to Kael. "You listen here, Kael Gardener. You do what you have to do and then we will deal with your mountain of bullshit when you're done. I meant what I said this morning. I love you. Now go do what you have to." She kissed him hard and handed Jagger her knife, but he refused to take her gun and vest, insisting she might need them and he was fine.

* * * * *

The walk back to the RV was relatively quick. The sounds in the earphones were bad so Alex took hers and swore he'd tell her if anything bad was happening to Kael.

"Con just showed up," Alex murmured to her as they approached the RV.

Inside, Minx was pacing, listening to the earphone, and Cap was awake and looking a lot better. Daniel was lying on the bed in the back, conscious, and his color was returning.

"Con said he had internal bleeding from the beating. He had bruises on his sides and back shaped like boots. Animals!" Lee exclaimed.

"Shit!" Minx and Alex both swore.

"What? Oh my god, are they okay?" Simone asked.

"Yes, but Anton is gone. They've gone through every room in the house and he's not there. Max is saying that sometimes the leader of the Oathbreaker group has a human whose sole job is to get him out in this kind of case," Alex said.

"We've seen it happen a few times before. They wrap the vampire in this funky lightproof cloth that zips up." Minx was silent as she listened to the comm link again. "They've gone to the front of the house. There are three cars and a space between two of them. They must have driven off in that."

Con shimmered into the RV. "Minx, you're to drive this to the mansion. Max is going to stay there so they can process the scene to see what evidence they can find. As Cap and

Daniel are fine and will recover, Kael wants them to stay resting but monitor the computers and comm link."

He turned to Alex, Em, Lee and Simone. "And you're all to go back to the house."

"What? He thinks he can just dump me off?" Simone was livid and heartbroken all at once.

Minx touched her arm. "No, Simone. There's hours of work to be done at the house. We have to see if we can find stuff like hair and skin for a DNA database we keep to see what vampires we've killed. That evidence may help us find Anton."

"Why don't we just drive now? Hit that road in Max's van to see if we can find the car!"

"Because we don't know what make the car was. We don't know when it left, and the highway is just a few minutes away. They could have had a safe residence nearby or they could be on their way out of state. We have no way of knowing right now. We've done this before, Simone. We know what we need to do now."

"And you'll come back to Lee's when you're done?"

"That would be my plan, yes."

Em took her hand and they were standing back in Lee's house then Con showed up with Lee and then went and got Alex.

Chapter Eight

ꝏ

Just before sundown Aidan and Connor came roaring downstairs, and finally Simone had to use the patented Charvez taxi hail whistle to get them to shut up. Connor headed out with the other Oathkeepers to join Max at the scene while Aidan stayed back with them to get an update.

Simone had no choice after so many hours of being awake and all of the drama of the last few days, and she went to bed after ordering them to wake her if anything important happened.

She woke up some hours later as the bed dipped. She smelled a freshly showered Kael.

"I was afraid you'd leave," she whispered.

"Can I lie down with you?" he asked.

"Please."

He lay down and pulled her to him, breathing her in, memorizing the way she felt against him. Warm and sexy and soft.

"I wouldn't just leave without saying goodbye."

"Oh."

He spoke, lips against her hair, "And I have to apologize for yesterday. I was afraid for my people and I took it out on you. It wasn't your fault. In fact, if you hadn't helped they'd all be dead. I'd probably be dead too. Or worse. Thank you for helping me even after I was so awful to you."

"Like I would have done anything else. Kael, get it through your thick head. I. Love. You. You needed help, your friends—my friends—were in danger and I helped. That's what you do for people you love. That's what family is. For better or worse."

His heart clenched in his chest at her words. God how he loved her and wanted a life with her. But what he'd done today had just proven how much his life was incompatible with hers. She wasn't meant to be in situations where people were murdered. She deserved to be free from danger.

"I don't need to be an empath to know you're thinking about being halfway out the door, Kael. What you aren't saying is just as telling as what you are saying."

"I can't! Damn it, Simone, I don't have anything for you. I can't give you what you deserve."

"And what is that? A man that I love? Someone with courage and compassion? Someone with a sense of justice and what is right? You are that man, Kael. Your sense of justice might be dark, but dark justice is better than none at all."

"I don't know what it is to be in a normal relationship. I see your family and I want it but it freaks me out too. I am too bent to be with anyone."

"Tell me. Tell me what happened to you. Tell me what made you this way." She didn't want to plead, but she didn't want him to leave either. She wanted him to understand just how much she loved him and what she was willing to go through. She was tough enough to be his woman.

He sighed and pulled her tighter against him. "It's not a happy story, Simone."

She snorted. "Well, I may not be a rocket scientist but I'd figured that much out."

"When I was six the vampires came. They broke through the front door, we were all in our family room watching a movie together. It was Friday. Popcorn and Kool-Aid night." His voice was distant as he remembered it, tried to disassociate himself from that boy long ago.

"My dad told me and my sister Gloria to hide. I was shoved under the couch but I could see the room. Gloria tried to get to the other room but they stopped her. I remember my dad pulled out a baseball bat and shouted at them as they swarmed into the room. They didn't move right. There was something...off...about how they came into the room. They laughed at my dad, who told them that he'd give them money and the keys to the cars if they just left.

"They killed him first. No ceremony. One moment he was standing there trying to protect us, the next he was looking down at the fist that had shoved through his chest. He saw me and mouthed *run*. But I couldn't.

"They took my mother and sister and tortured them both. There was so much blood. God. It was everywhere. Their eyes glowed. They had sharp white teeth. The screams and then the awful gurgles as they died.

"I crawled out from under the couch and to my mother but I was covered with blood and in shock. When they did see me I was frozen in fear. I think they thought I was dead, and there were so many of them and so much death and mayhem that no one gave it a second thought."

He told her about the foster mother who'd reared him and Jagger. About how he started hunting at fifteen. About Charity and Mexico.

"No wonder you hated them so much that you didn't want to believe any of them were good like Aidan. But now that you know you were wrong, now that you know there are good vampires, surely you can let go of this and let yourself love." Simone held his face between her palms.

"I don't know what to think about it all. But I know I can't think about it here. Not with you. Siren, you steal my edge. I need that edge to keep my people alive."

She sat up, pulled her shirt off and knelt before him. "You're going to walk out on me?" Her voice was thick with tears. She kicked off her panties and shook her hair out. "You'd walk away from this? From this thing between us? So you can keep killing vampires? You can't do both?"

He came to his knees and she saw how hard he was. He moved so that he was touching her, body to body. His cock burned against her stomach. "You think I want to leave?" He grabbed her hair and pulled her head back and his lips crushed hers. He ate her up, devoured her lips. His tongue plundered her mouth, tasted her, committed her to memory to play back that moment over and over until he was no more. Her taste burned into him, flooded his senses. She was so right in his arms.

"God, I want you so much. I've never wanted anything like the way I want you," he whispered against her lips.

"I'm yours, Kael. Take me. Own me. Own *us*. Know that you can be with me, come to me, find comfort and solace and strength in me. Because I am yours. And you are mine." Simone poured all of her love for him into her words, into her hands and her eyes, into her lips as she kissed him. Every cell in her body, every bit of her very soul wanted to heal this man. Wanted to heal *her* man and create a life with him. She wanted to be the person that gave him pause enough to reject this vendetta and embrace his future.

"Oh man," he moaned and kissed her chin. He laid small, hot kisses across her jaw and up toward her ear. His tongue dipped into that delicate shell and it brought an eruption of shivers of delight over her body.

His palms slid up and cupped her breasts, pulled lightly on her nipples. Her head fell back at the delicious sensation as her own hands moved over the muscled wall of his chest and up his neck into his hair. She held him to her body as he kissed down the line of her neck and over the curve of her shoulder.

The scent of her skin tantalized him, touched him deep in a place he'd kept walled off for far too long. She was warm and pliant in his arms, giving him everything she had to offer and more. She held nothing back, but rather laid herself bare and utterly vulnerable before him. The depth of that, of her courage and honesty—of her love for him—humbled him and made him realize that Simone Charvez was much more courageous than anyone he'd ever met before.

"I need to taste all of you, siren. Lie back."

Her passion-blurred eyes focused a bit and she lay back, still looking up at him, wearing the smile of a fallen angel. Her sex goddess body writhed beneath his gaze and his body.

He swirled the point of his tongue around her straining nipple and she gasped, fingers gripping the sheet. She wrapped a calf around him to pull him closer and he felt the heat of her.

The edge of his teeth scraped along the tip of her nipple and she moaned his name. He rained small kisses down the curve of one breast and up the other, finding the nipple with lips, teeth and tongue.

Each draw of his mouth reverberated through her body, her clit throbbed in time and her heart seemed to pound in rhythm.

Her hands skimmed down the hard muscles of his back and over his amazing ass. She arched into him to rub herself against him, unashamedly pulling more pleasure from the moment. He brought her so much physical joy. The way he touched her, it was like the one thing that he allowed himself to fully express the depth of his feelings for her. When he was making love to her she could see the real Kael, feel his vulnerability and his caring and his love for her. He didn't have to say the words—she could feel it at that very moment.

He kissed his way down her stomach and she parted her thighs. He looked up at her and she gasped softly at the raw emotion on his face.

"Hold yourself open for me," he coaxed and she reached down, parting her sex for him. "Oh, siren. You have such a pretty pussy. You're all swollen and wet for me. I can't wait to lap up all that cream."

He leaned in and took a long, swirling lick from her gate up around her clit and she mewled at the pleasure of it. Over and over he took long licks, his tongue parting the folds of her pussy, the tip flicking over her clit. All while she held herself open to him and his erotic assault.

Each slide of his tongue through her pussy pushed her closer and closer to orgasm. The way that he touched her, seared into her soul—the gentleness of his hands on her hips, tilting her body up to him, serving himself with her made her feel loved.

The slow journey through this pleasurable experience was all-encompassing. Everything was Kael, the way he made her feel physically and emotionally. His scent. His hands on her body. The sound of his voice, of his breathing. He filled her up and made her whole and when her climax broke it rushed over her body, through her senses, leaving every nerve endings tingling and sparking with sensation.

He crawled up her body until his lips hovered just above hers. Eyes open, gazing deep into her soul, he kissed her with such softness, such yearning and love that it brought tears to her eyes.

She took his face in her hands, holding him like the precious thing he was. For all his guns and knives and warrior ways, he was so vulnerable, so wounded and hurt. Simone just wanted to heal that pain, to fill up the empty spots inside him and make him whole as well.

She started to speak but he put a finger over her lips. "No, please. Siren, don't say anything. Let's just be. I need so very much to be inside of you. Let me make love to you, please."

She nodded, swallowing her words, and opened her thighs in invitation.

But he got up and held out a hand. She took it, a question in her eyes. "Put your hands on the dresser there and bend forward. I want to take you from behind but I want to see your face when I do it."

There were mirrors hanging behind the dresser, and a free-standing mirror next to them. She shivered at his request and did it, looking up at his reflection as she complied.

He knelt and ran his hands up her legs and stood as he did it. Gently, he widened her thighs and Simone watched in the mirrors as he took his cock in his hand and guided it to her pussy.

Fascinated, as if it were something she was watching on television, she watched as he pushed into her body. She watched that woman in the mirror tilt her hips back to take him deeper. Watched the blur of passion film his eyes.

His thrusts were slow and deep. He savored each movement into her body and then out again. Simone saw the sweep of his palms down her back and up again, over her shoulders and down her arms. His hands gathered her hair and pulled. Not too hard but hard enough to let her know he was running the show. That brought a shiver of need up her spine.

"Oh, siren, you feel so good around my cock. Like you were meant for me. I never want this to end."

She met his gaze in the mirror directly in front of her but didn't say what she knew she told him with her eyes. That she was meant for him, that it didn't have to end. She knew he wouldn't hear it—that he knew it but couldn't face it.

Instead, she thrust herself back at him, never taking her gaze from his. He moved his hands around and cupped her breasts as he moved, flicking his thumbs up and over her nipples, his hands large and battle-hardened and yet gentle on her soft skin. She gasped as he pinched her nipples and slid one hand down to her pussy, finding her clit.

"You're not wet enough," he murmured and watched as his hand rose up and she took his fingers into her mouth for a few moments to get them wet. His cock jumped inside her at the sight.

"Jesus, you're sexy."

She gave him a wry smile.

Slowly, his fingers circled her clit as he fucked into her body. The threads that bound them together formed tighter and tighter and yet, Simone feared, not tight enough. There was this synchronicity between them. As a couple they filled the room with magic.

She knew he was nearing climax as his breath got shallow and the digs of his cock sped up. His fingers on her clit increased in speed but kept a gentle touch. He knew what she liked.

"Come for me, siren. Come with me," he whispered as he leaned in.

His words pulled her over and she took him with her as her cunt clenched and fluttered around him in the beginnings of her orgasm.

He pressed into her as deep as he could and she watched the muscles on his neck cord as he came, felt each jerk of his cock as his hands moved back to her hips and held her to his body through the throes of his climax.

"Oooh, Simone. God, I..." he broke off before he told her he loved her and she sighed. It was then that she realized he wasn't wearing a condom and she was very glad she was on the Pill and hoped he didn't make not wearing any protection a habit.

He moved back and made a sound of discovery. "Oh shit, I wasn't wearing protection."

She turned to him. "I'm on the Pill. I hope unprotected sex isn't a regular thing with you."

"No. God, I'd never risk you like that."

She raised a brow but didn't say anything. "I'm going to take a shower."

"You want some help scrubbing your back?" He grinned at her.

She didn't have the energy to pretend her world wasn't falling apart. "No. I need to think." She turned and walked into the bathroom and shut the door behind herself.

Kael knew he'd hurt her, knew that she'd stiffened when he pulled back from saying he loved her. He'd wanted to so badly but he just couldn't.

He got into bed and waited for her. He hoped that when she came out she'd dump him. That would make it easier on both of them. He could leave and make a clean break. He didn't know if he had the strength to refuse if she begged him to stay.

She came out of the bathroom and the sight of her broke his heart. He realized she was dressed in street clothes and he sat up.

"Siren?"

She waved him back and sat down at the foot of the bed. "I need to say this so please don't interrupt me." She took a deep breath and looked him square in the eyes.

"I'm giving you something that I didn't know if I'd have the strength to do. I'm giving you a choice. You can choose me. Choose us. Build a life with me here in New Orleans or heck, just about anywhere. I'm willing to be with you wherever, whenever. You can choose to let go of that terrified little boy and of all that pain and vengeance. Rule it instead of letting it rule you.

"I love you. I believe you love me. I would do just about anything for you to help you. If you want to continue hunting, I'll come on the road with you. As you know, in my world there are people who are meant for each other. It isn't always a one true mate situation like it is with Em and Con or a magical triad like it is with Lee and her men. Sometimes though, you are meant to fit with another person. You are that fit for me.

"But I cannot…I will not live with a man who is only half a person because he only allows himself to feel the negative emotions and walls out love and commitment because he's afraid. Oh don't get that look—you are afraid. You're afraid to love me and have me die like your family, like Charity, like the other members of your crew who have died."

"Simone, don't presume..."

"Shut up, Kael. I'm talking and when I'm done you can go back to living in denial but I won't have it right now." She shot him a glare and he snorted but closed his mouth.

"Now, as I was saying—you can choose me and being with me. Let yourself love me and let me love you. Or, you can choose to walk away. I won't chase you or beg you. That's not fair to either of us and I don't want you to be with me for any other reason but your choosing to do so. But I won't wait around forever. I have to move forward with my life and heal. That may mean at some point in the future I'll have to let go of you and look for love elsewhere. I want a family, I want a relationship. He'll have to be good man who knows that there will always be another in my heart, because Kael, no matter what, I will always love you. But I won't play second best to your need to hunt down vampires because you feel guilty you didn't help your parents fight off vampires when you were six."

Kael flinched. "That's not fair. Don't psychoanalyze me!"

"Fine. I think you've made your choice but I'm going to go now. I'll give you some time to really think this over. If you haven't darkened my doorway by the end of the week, I'll assume you chose your vengeance instead of love and hope."

She stood and he went to her. "Where are you going? Anton is still out there somewhere! At least stay with me for a while."

Simone shook her head and leaned in to kiss him and hold him tight against her body, letting herself get lost in the intensity of her love for him for just a few moments more. "What? You thought you'd be the one to walk out on me when you were done?" She stepped back. "I'm not your responsibility, Kael Gardener. Where I go is my business. You can choose to make it yours but I'm not a burden for you to bear along with that giant cross you carry." She reached for the doorknob, praying he'd stop her and make his choice right then but he didn't say anything.

"You're welcome to stay here for as long as you wish. Lee wanted me to be sure to tell you that. Goodbye, Kael. If I don't see you again, remember that someone in New Orleans loves you and cares about you more than life. Be safe."

She turned and walked out, shutting the door firmly behind her. She made it to the stairs before the tears started. Gratefully, she saw Em standing down below waiting for her.

* * * * *

Kael watched Simone leave the room and felt his world fall out from under his feet. He had to sit down before he fell down. His heart wanted to run after her and choose her. Damn it, how dare she give him a choice instead of an ultimatum? What she'd done was selfless and loving and he adored her even more for it.

He sat there in the bed where he'd loved her and taken her love. Their mingled scents hung in the air. One of her hairclips was on the nightstand and he reached out and picked it up, thinking.

As he'd made love to her, he'd allowed himself to imagine a life with her. A life where he had a home. A real home with a front porch and a kitchen and a big willow tree out front. The feel of her body beneath his own, around his own, next to his own, was something that drew him out of the world where he felt nothing and into a place where he felt like there was hope for himself.

Simone was real and now. She offered him a path away from what he was quickly becoming. At the same time, he worried that she took his edge. Already he wanted to hunt less. He owed it to his parents to keep going.

With a groan, he got up and put his clothes back on. Grabbing his bag and putting her hairclip in a pocket, he walked quickly and resolutely out of the house, got on his motorcycle and drove away.

He got back to their rental house and couldn't resist a look across the way to Simone's. The shades were drawn in Simone's bedroom but open in the living room. He hated the idea of her being alone with Anton still out there and resolved to talk with Connor about it before they left town.

The house was quiet when he walked in. Everyone had been up all night processing the mansion and he figured they were all resting. Cap was dealing with his injuries and the loss of yet more family to the vampires. Daniel would recover slowly but he would live.

He crawled into his bed and reached for that place where he felt nothing, and its familiar comfort lulled him to sleep.

* * * * *

"Come on, *bébé*. Let me take you home." Em held out her hand to Simone, who took it with a sob, and they shimmered back into Simone's apartment.

Instead of just creating tea like Con would have, Em preferred the comfort of making it. She bustled around the kitchen in the mid-morning light getting everything ready, and finally turned and sat down at the table while the tea steeped.

"So. Tell me."

Simone told her cousin everything about the choice she'd given Kael. About how she'd had one small shred of hope until he'd pulled back from saying he loved her. About how she'd stood in the shower and debated just what to do but in the end realized that she had to choose self-respect and dignity and let Kael choose her or not, and that she had to walk away on her terms or she'd hate herself and he'd resent her.

Em nodded as she drank her tea. "Well, for what it's worth, I think you did the right thing. He has to come to you freely, he has to reject this millstone of hatred that's enslaved him to this fear of loving someone. You don't need to live that way. I just wish this was easier for you. I wish I could fix it. It pains me to see you hurting so much."

Simone smiled through her tears. "Thanks, little raven. But you know," she shrugged, "it'll either happen or it won't. I can't do anything about it at this stage and so I need to move on and get on with my life and hope like hell he wises up. Because if he thinks he can reject me and sleep around with truck stop chippies, he'd better think again! I'll curse him so his pecker falls off!"

Em burst out laughing. "There's my girl!"

"I'll arrange it with Connor to deal with what I'll do about Anton. If he's still out there I'll need protection or something. I should use the link to see where he is now. He'll have awakened and been to sleep by this point." Simone saw the look on Em's face and laughed. "But I know I shouldn't do it without all of us fully rested and at Lee's, where the protection is strongest. Don't worry."

"Okay, then. Why don't you sleep now? I'll stay here until you wake up."

Simone realized how bone tired she was and nodded. "Okay. Thank you, *chère*."

Em stood up and hugged her tight. "Of course, that's what family is for, yes?"

Simone nodded wearily, shuffled into the bedroom and fell onto the bed and into sleep within moments.

Em called Max and explained the situation to him. He said he'd arrange with Connor to have someone with Simone at all times and that they should come back to the house that night to work on plans for the future.

"He's gone."

"Kael left already?" Em's heart sank.

"Yes. Shortly after you two left he stormed out. You should know that Connor offered to make him and his hunters human liaison members to the Oathkeepers. A good salary, great equipment. Stability, Em. He could hunt still, but with the power of the vampire nation behind him and on a schedule. He wouldn't have to drive around all the time. He could have a home if he chose."

"Damn that man! What is wrong with him? All of this staring him in the face and he walks away? A woman like Simone, a whole woman who loves him and wants him, darkness and all. A chance at something of a normal life. I don't get it."

"Em, if I may, he's terrified. I spent a lot of time with him when we dealt with the mansion. He told me about what happened to him at the hands of the Oathbreakers. If he loves Simone back, he feels like he's endangering her. If he stops hunting he feels like he's turned his back on his mission to hunt down the things that killed his family. If he lets go of what's been the mainstay of his life since the age of six, what then? Can you imagine? What a scary thing, to leap into something totally unknown. I envy him Simone, but I don't envy him the courage it'll take to make the right choice here."

"You're a smart man, Max."

"I know you thought I was all brawn and no brains. But I hear a lot. I watch and learn."

"What do you think he'll do?"

"I don't know, Em. I mean, he's a brave man without a doubt. He's strong, and although he's an ass, he's smart. I just don't know if he'll make the best choice here."

Em let out a breath and thanked Max before hanging up. Con came to join her and they talked and snuggled while watching old movies and trying not to think about the heartbreak Simone was facing.

Chapter Nine

Connor had barely held his rage in check when he'd found out Kael hadn't taken Simone's love. A woman like Simone was a once-in-a-lifetime blessing and the human had just tossed it away like she didn't matter. He just couldn't understand it and he ached for the pain he saw in her eyes.

He also couldn't help but wonder what Melanie was going to do. It was impossible for him to think of her as Minx, even though she was sexy as hell. After talking to her and getting to know her, she was Melanie to him. He wondered where she'd go now. He wanted to be with her when all of this madness wasn't going on because he was strongly attracted to her in a way that made the way he'd felt about females before her seem pale and watery.

"I'm not going to do that!" Simone exclaimed, bringing Connor out of his thoughts and back to the task at hand, dealing with the very real issue of Simone's safety. Her entire family had gathered and each one of them made a go at trying to get her to see reason. It wasn't working.

"Minnie, you're not being reasonable. You *know* this vampire is out to get you. Why on earth would you tempt danger this way? Live here with us for the time being. You don't need to work in the shop, you can have clients come here." Lee pleaded with Simone, but Simone had a granite-hard set to her chin and even Connor, someone relatively new to her life, knew that look.

"Lee, don't think that I don't appreciate that. I really do. But I will not let Anton Perdue drive me away from my dreams! He's already taken Kael from me, I won't let him take my shop and my business too. I will live in my home and work in my building. Period. We've got great warding there and we know it works. I won't be stupid. I'll stay in at night. But I can't stop living."

"Simone, let us put some guards on you then. Max will stay with you during the days and I'll have one of our vampires guard you at night. Once we get a lock on Perdue and kill him you'll be free. But until then, you'll be safe and everyone will feel a lot better about it." Connor fought to keep his tone reasonable. If he sounded remotely authoritarian, she'd balk.

"Speaking of that, let's use the link to see where he is. I'll take you up on the offer of the guards, by the way. I may be independent but I'm not stupid."

"Simone, *bébé,* are you sure you're up to this?" Lou sounded anxious.

"What other choice is there? Should I wait around and let things happen to me or should I just make them happen for myself?" Simone exploded and stood up. She put her hands over her face for a moment and took a deep breath. "I apologize, *Maman*. I shouldn't have spoken to you that way. I just need to be in control of this. We have this weapon, let's use it."

Lou went to Simone and hugged her tight. "It's okay, I know you're hurting."

They filed into the drawing room and formed a circle. Simone, Em and Lee in one. Isolde, Marie and Lou outside that—creating two concentric circles. Alex, Con, Connor and Aidan made the four corners of the connection.

Simone went deep and followed that sick thread that tied her to Anton but felt nothing. After a few more minutes she gave up.

"Nothing. Do you think that means he's dead?" she asked hopefully.

"I think you'd have felt that," Connor thought about it. "No, I think he's just far away physically."

"Really? Like out of state? Out of the country?"

"Well, he favors Mexico and Italy. Our people have been watching the airports and borders but we can't watch every mile of the border with Mexico and from there he could fly anywhere. We'll have to widen our net now."

"Does this mean I'm safe?"

"For the time being. But if he can get out of the country in less than twenty-four hours, he can get back. So don't relax your vigilance, Simone."

"Great," she mumbled.

They ate a family dinner and Con shimmered her and Max and her vampire guard back to her house sometime in the late night.

She made up a bedroom for both men and insisted that they make themselves at home. "As long as you're here, this is your home too."

* * * * *

Kael woke up and trudged out to the kitchen, realizing it had been well over twenty-four hours since he'd eaten last.

"You want to tell me what the hell you're doing here instead of across the street?" Jagger demanded as he walked into the room.

"You know the situation, Jagger. She's not for me. It was never a permanent thing. She'll move on. It's better this way."

"Better for who?" Jagger folded himself into a chair. "Better for you and the soulless monster you seem to want to be? What the fuck kind of person are you trying to make yourself?"

"I don't need your shit right now, Jagger."

"The hell you don't, boyo! You've never needed it more. I haven't said much as this whole situation unfolded. I've watched you, watched her, watched the two of you together. She's the light to your darkness, Kael. You have a chance here, a chance to be more than a killing machine. She can save you from that. Are you so afraid of letting go of your hatred so you can love that you'll just let her slip away?"

"Hey, fuck you. What do you know about it?" Kael snarled, the pointed barbs Jagger had sent striking straight in his heart.

Jagger took a deep breath and Kael heard his breath hitch. "I know that if I had the chance to be with Charity again I'd take it. If I had the chance to feel that kind of love and connection to my woman, I'd grab it and not look back. Charity made me a complete person, Kael. Simone does that for you."

"What if I do want to look back, huh? I'm a hunter, I don't just stop being a hunter because I'm in love!" Kael stood up and began to pace.

Minx watched from the doorway. "You don't have to. Take the job with the Oathkeepers. Let New Orleans be our base of operations. We can be a hundred times more effective with their resources. That and have roots! My god, it's been so damned long since I've had a home. Eight years of being on the road three hundred and sixty five days a year. Of hotels being what I yearn for so I can sleep in a bed that doesn't move. To have the tiniest bit of privacy."

Jagger was silent for long moments as he waited for it all to sink in with Kael. "She doesn't expect you to give up being a hunter. She just expects you to give it up as your all-encompassing need. This thing with the Oathkeepers is good for all of us. I'm tired, Kael. I want a little apartment of my own. I want to walk to the market every day and have a coffee shop where they know my name. I want a bank account and a bed and art on my walls. I still want to hunt down the evil bastards that killed my parents and my wife, but I want a life. This has been my existence for fifteen years and I've been a hunter my entire life. I want more." Jagger said the last in a very quiet voice.

"I love you, Kael. You are my brother and my best friend. Simone Charvez is a dream come true. Not only is she incredible to look at but she's strong and smart and willing to put up with your shit. She isn't asking a lot here. But she's right. Let it go and be a whole person. Be a part of something more than this hunt for death."

"What about Cap and Daniel?"

"They want to stay too. We've all talked and wanted to approach you as soon as this was over. But don't do this for us. Do it for you," Minx said softly.

"I have to think. I'm going for a ride." Kael picked up his keys and his helmet and left.

He drove for hours, until he ended up at the ocean. It was after dark, and he checked in at a small motel on the water and went in search of some dinner.

Sitting there at the oceanfront restaurant, drinking a beer and listening to the ocean, he wrestled with his competing responsibilities.

"Is this seat taken?"

Kael looked up the long body of the most striking woman he'd ever clapped eyes on. Her long, white-blonde hair flowed freely and appeared to have feathers woven in it that gently moved in the breeze. Her eyes were an otherworldly blue. She wasn't beautiful, beautiful was too simple a word for what she was. No, the woman before him was simply perfect. Certainly sexy and alluring. And yet, while three months ago he'd have pursued her until they ended up in bed, she did nothing for him. All he wanted was Simone.

"Uh, no thanks. I mean, you're quite lovely and all, but I have someone."

She laughed, a beautiful melody of sound, and sat anyway, crossing her long legs and dangling a sandal from one perfect foot. "Well, I'm glad you realize that. I suppose that's one thing at least."

"Huh?"

She held out her hand. "I'm Freya and I'm here to save that very well-toned butt of yours."

"Do I know you?"

She rolled her eyes and took his beer and drank it as if it were hers. "I'm a friend of all Charvez women. And right now, I'm going to do you the biggest favor of your life. What are you doing here? She is back in New Orleans alone and missing you and you are here? Listening to the ocean and thinking about the long dead?"

He stiffened. "Who are you? How did you know that? Did Simone send you?"

"You're not very bright, are you? Let's start again. I'm Freya. I'm what some believe to be a goddess, others believe me an angel. I am a being of light and magic and sorcery. I am she who crafted the Compact which gives your Simone her gift of feeling."

He widened his eyes and she laughed again. He had to admit it was as perfect as the rest of her. "Goddesses too? Just when I think I've seen it all."

She nodded. "And you don't even know the half of what exists in the universe. But that's neither here nor there. You must know that Simone would never divulge your story of your childhood to a total stranger. I highly doubt she'd even tell her family without your permission."

"And so you know I'm thinking about the long dead how? That she's back in New Orleans how? Anything at all about me how?"

She widened her eyes at him. "Shall we revisit the part where I told you I am a goddess? I know many things, Kael. I know that your mother named you Kael because she knew when she carried you that you'd be a warrior of some kind. It came to her in a dream. I know that your father died with love for all of you in his heart. I know that they would not want you to carry them around for this many years as a reason to shut the most wondrous thing that will ever happen to you out of your heart."

"I owe them!"

"You don't owe them the way you believe you do. You owe it to them to be happy and to let yourself love."

He stood up and tossed some money on the table. "You don't know anything," he snarled and stalked out of the restaurant and down onto the sand.

She was sitting on the deck chair outside his room when he got back, silvery blonde hair gleaming in the moonlight. There were two very large cats purring at her feet as she idly scratched their heads.

"I know that you are a fool of the highest order if you let Simone Charvez get away. She loves you. She loves you with a strength and purity that is so rare that I can count the number of times I've seen it over my lifetime on my fingers." She spoke as if their conversation at the restaurant had never been interrupted.

"Damn it! I can't!" He stomped into the room and she followed and perched on the dresser.

"You're afraid to lose her."

He opened his mouth to deny it but closed it again. "Can you guarantee that I won't?"

"No. I don't have that kind of power over life and death and there are dangerous beings that concern themselves with both you and Simone. There are no guarantees in life, not even for me. But the real question to ask yourself, Kael, is whether it's worth it enough to risk that, to risk losing her to have her. You cannot have both. You have to open your hands to grasp and in doing so, you chance dropping it. Can you imagine a future without Simone in it? A future where she smiles at another man over the breakfast table? Hmm?"

He slumped back to the bed. "I'm so fucking tired of being afraid."

She approached him with a soft smile. Brushing her fingertips over his brow, she murmured, "I know. Let her share your burden. Glow with her, Kael Gardener."

* * * * *

It had been a hard night and an even harder morning as Simone had to force herself to get used to Kael's absence. She'd given him until the end of the week but with each passing hour she felt less and less hope that he'd come to her. Two days had passed and nothing.

She'd seen Minx and they'd chatted briefly, with Minx saying that she truly hoped Kael would come to his senses and take the job and stay in New Orleans with Simone. Casually, but oh-so obviously, Minx asked after Connor, who'd had to travel to Atlanta to meet with some other Oathkeepers about Anton.

"He feels a deep attraction to you, you know." Simone's heart was heavy but her tone was light. She smiled at Minx, hoping that one of them at least, had a happy ending.

"The feeling is mutual. I just want to rip his clothes off and jump him and then make him a sandwich! It's so not like me."

They'd laughed and she'd asked Minx what she planned to do in the future. "I won't leave Kael. I prefer to take this liaison job but if he wants to leave I'll go with him. He's family to me."

Simone was glad for it, glad to know that he'd have someone with him to care about him and love him if he chose to leave.

On the fourth day, when Minx reported that he hadn't come back from his ride, Simone began to worry that something had happened to him. While she could believe he'd leave New Orleans without anything else to say to her, she couldn't believe he wouldn't at least tell his crew.

She was in the back of the shop mixing a new batch of lemonade when she heard the chimes on the door.

"I'll be with you in just a moment!" she called as she brought the tray out. She placed it on the large desk, looked up with a smile and nearly fell over.

"Kael!" She wanted to run to him, but at the same time she couldn't bear it if he didn't return her embrace. But there he was, all menace and blond good looks with that bad boy edge. She loved him so much that it rushed through her with bittersweet intensity that this might be the last time she laid eyes on him.

"Siren. I'm sorry I've been gone so long." He walked toward her, holding out his hands and she moved to him slowly, taking them but not embracing him.

"I was worried that you hadn't checked in. I was worried Anton had gotten you or you were hurt somewhere and all alone," she whispered, looking up into those blue eyes that held so much pain and yet…

He smiled. "Can I kiss you, siren? 'Cause you look damned good and I want a taste."

She nodded, still mesmerized by his eyes. His kiss was the gentlest brush of lips across hers. The familiar scent of him settled over her as his beard tickled her chin.

"Now I'm going to talk and you're going to listen, got me?"

She raised an eyebrow but stayed quiet.

"I love you."

The sound of those words burst over her, roared through her heart, filled her with joy and she wanted to whoop in the most unladylike way but she just smiled at him and waited for him to continue.

"That was easier than I thought. Okay, so anyway, first Lee went at me at the mansion. Then Jagger and Minx at the house. There was so much I had to deal with, mull over. All of this competing stuff. Fear of losing you and fear of grabbing you. Fear of letting go of the rage that's kept me going all these years. Anyway, I went to the shore to think and then I met this woman in the bar and *ouch*! Let me finish! Sheesh, you're a jealous one." He rubbed the spot on his inner arm where she'd pinched him.

"You'd best remember that, Kael Gardener," she growled.

He laughed. "Siren, the woman in the bar was your Freya. She talked to me, said things, told me things, helped me let go of things that had been holding me back. I woke up the next morning and headed to Atlanta.

"It took me some time and some negotiation but I took Connor's offer of being a human liaison team to the Oathkeepers. I wanted to be back before now but I had to negotiate our position and meet all sorts of people. Vampires."

"What does this mean, Kael?" she asked carefully. She wanted to be absolutely sure of what was happening before she let herself get too happy.

"It means I choose us." He knelt before her and put his arms around her waist. "I love you, Simone. I want to be with you. I want to wake up with you and listen to you yammer on endlessly about what color toenail polish you should wear. I want to be your family."

She closed her eyes and held his head to her.

"I can't give up hunting altogether, though. It's what I know, what I do. Can you live with that?" He tipped his head back and looked up at her.

"I can. I never expected you to stop altogether. I know you have a job to do and it's your driving passion. I respect that. Heck, you should have a witch as a member of your team. I can help so much!"

"No. It's dangerous." He stood and went toe-to-toe with her.

She kissed him. "You love me."

He smiled. "I do. And do you still love me?"

"You're as dumb as a stump sometimes. Of course I do."

"Then close up for a bit and come across the way with me while I tell the rest of the team about the deal I just made. Believe it or not, I got the vampire nation to give us a house! I would consider it an honor if you and your family would ward it so we can live safely. The vamps are even going to provide my crew with the best high-tech gear and… Oh, and Simone?"

"Of course we'll ward it! Will everyone live there? I don't mind really as long as we have some privacy and I have a workspace."

"Simone?"

"Hmm?"

"You and I have something else to take care of."

"What's that? God, don't tell me there are more dark secrets!"

"No. You just need to marry me and make me legal so your mom and brothers won't think I'm some floozy out to corrupt their daughter. I don't care where or when, I'll let you deal with that stuff. But I did pick this up when I was in Atlanta." He pulled a simple band out of his pocket.

"The symbols are the same runic protection symbols on my body. Well, the ones on my chest and over your door. There's diamonds too, but you don't get those rings until you make me legal." He slid the ring on her finger and she closed her eyes as the overwhelming sense of rightness settled over her. Breathing out, she fully allowed herself to love this man, to feel that joy that he brought into her life.

"In reply to your ever-so-unconventional proposal, I say yes. And I will indeed plan and you'd better not run off too many times and interrupt my time line." She narrowed her eyes and put her hands on her hips. "Oh, and I love the ring, it's very beautiful and very special."

He let out a sigh of relief. "Whew! I was worried." He held out his hand. "Shall we go talk to the crew?"

She flipped over the open sign and called out, "Max, I'll be back in a while. I'm going across the way!"

"I know. I'm just in the other room, remember. You're lucky you came to your senses Gardener, now I won't have to kill you."

Kael laughed and then sobered up. "We'll talk about your safety issues too. Connor told me about the Anton situation."

She tugged his arm, not toward the street but the stairs up to her apartment. Her smile was the one he'd come to love so much—sex personified.

"Oh it's like that?"

She laughed, low and seductive. "Oh yeah. Like that and then some. Your crew will have to wait a while."

Scooping her up into his arms, he took the stairs two at a time, opened the door and slammed it with the kick of his boot heel. He didn't stop walking until he reached her bedroom and tossed her on the bed.

Kael didn't fail to notice the lines of sadness around her eyes. Ripping his shirt off, he fell to the bed and kissed her face gently, over and over. "I'm sorry I hurt you. You're right, I was scared. Love me, Simone."

It rushed through her then, the enormity of his words. He'd made himself vulnerable to her and she didn't feel so alone anymore. Pushing up off the bed, she fell to her knees and he sat up.

Looking up at him, her eyes met his. His pupils widened and his lips slightly parted.

With a smile, she reached out and unzipped and unbuttoned his jeans and he lifted up enough for her to pull them off his body. It was then that she took his cock into her hands. He was so alive, hot and hard, the vein throbbing under her thumb.

Leaning in, she slowly drew her cheek over that velvety flesh. The heat of him against her face was intoxicating. The scent of his body, the musk that identified him as *hers* made her body respond as their chemicals danced together.

The tip of her tongue found a path from his balls to that slit, already glistening with pre-cum. Unable to stop herself, she took a lick, tasting him, bringing his essence into her body.

"Simone, my sweet siren, you're killing me. Please."

With a brief smile, she opened her mouth enough to admit the head and she swirled her tongue around the crown. The texture of his skin changed as he hardened even more. Knowing she affected him so deeply made her wet and achy for him.

Slowly, Simone slid her mouth down over the length of his cock, taking him in as deeply as she could. Dreamily, she began a slow rhythm of up and down, teasing licks and nibbles, seducing him toward climax. Each time she swallowed him into her body, it was another step closer.

Her hands held his thighs and she felt the trembling and tightening of the muscles. Opening her eyes, she looked up his body and met his gaze. Got caught in the hunger in his eyes as he watched her.

That moment made her feel like a goddess. Like the sexiest siren that ever lived. He saw her as something beautiful and desirable. He *knew* her and wanted her. And she knew that. She didn't need to be an empath to know it, she could see it in the way he looked at her.

And moments later in the way gentle hands pulled her off his cock. "Siren, I'm very close to coming and I want to, no, I *need* to be inside you when I do. Come and ride me."

Scrambling back onto the bed, she straddled his body and kissed over the runes on his chest, pressing her lips over his heart. His reverent hands slid over her body as he helped divest her of her clothing.

She'd never needed anything more than she needed him to be inside her. With her panties still clinging to one ankle, she pulled up enough to reach and guide him true, sinking down onto his cock with a soft moan of satisfaction.

"Fuck. Oh you feel so damned good, siren. I've missed you so much."

How long had she waited for this? There was no way to know how good it made her feel. She knew she'd have more work on her hands, it wasn't like he could be totally open overnight, but he'd given her such a gift of love and trust.

"I missed you too. I thought I'd die when I walked out of that room. I stood at the top of the stairs willing you to come out. And the days passed and I thought you'd gone and more days passed and I began to worry that something had happened to you. And now you're here. I love you, Kael."

He struggled back to sitting, making sure to stay deep within her. "Now I can touch you better, kiss you more." And making good on that comment, his lips found hers. His tongue stroked over the seam of her lips and she opened to him with a sigh, shivering as he flowed into her mouth.

For long minutes there was nothing more than carnal kisses, the soft stroke of hands on flesh and the barest undulation of her body over his. The heat built until Kael broke the kiss and gasped. "I can't be slow anymore, siren."

"Show me what you've got."

With a laugh, he quickly moved and tossed her on her back as he loomed over her body. "You're on."

Long, hard strokes of his cock deep into her body made her writhe beneath him. Her hips rolled up to meet his thrusts. He felt her pussy clench around him and it shot straight to his balls.

"I don't have any hands free, siren. Make yourself come for me. I'll owe you one and you can make me pay you back in all manner of dirty, naughty ways later when I have feeling in my lower body again."

Her eyes locked with his, she moved her hand down to her clit, pushing past it to where they were joined, gathering her honey and bringing it back up. "It won't be long, I'm so close."

"I want you to come. I want to feel you come around me." He saw the naked need on her face and had to kiss her again. Couldn't get enough of her taste. Couldn't make it real enough that he'd chosen this woman who loved him despite what he was, and in doing so made him a better man.

Her teeth caught his lower lip and her back arched. Her cunt fluttered and then spasmed around his cock and it shot up his spine. He pressed deep once, twice and a last time as he came, pouring himself into her.

She swallowed the low sound he made as he let go of the pain and the fear and embraced all she meant to his life. What she gave back was acceptance. She took the demons and gave him love. No, she took the demons, fought them at his side, and gave him love.

After he'd come, he pressed his forehead to hers. "I'm such a lucky man."

She nodded solemnly. "You are. And don't forget it."

* * * * *

It was an hour later when they found their way out of the apartment and out of the store. The heat hit them like a fist but she didn't look the slightest bit bothered by it. He shook his head, amused.

"After we let ourselves enjoy this for a bit, I'm going to have to find a way to thank Freya. She's gotten my family out of a few binds in the last few years."

"Yes, after we enjoy this for a bit more. Naked and sweaty," he said in an undertone and put his arm around her shoulder. He felt free in a way he couldn't remember ever feeling. Free of his incessant need for vengeance, free of his fear. Simone's love had done that and he planned to thank her for it every day for the rest of his life.

Why an electronic book?

We live in the Information Age—an exciting time in the history of human civilization, in which technology rules supreme and continues to progress in leaps and bounds every minute of every day. For a multitude of reasons, more and more avid literary fans are opting to purchase e-books instead of paper books. The question from those not yet initiated into the world of electronic reading is simply: *Why?*

1. ***Price.*** An electronic title at Ellora's Cave Publishing and Cerridwen Press runs anywhere from 40% to 75% less than the cover price of the exact same title in paperback format. Why? Basic mathematics and cost. It is less expensive to publish an e-book (no paper and printing, no warehousing and shipping) than it is to publish a paperback, so the savings are passed along to the consumer.
2. ***Space.*** Running out of room in your house for your books? That is one worry you will never have with electronic books. For a low one-time cost, you can purchase a handheld device specifically designed for e-reading. Many e-readers have large, convenient screens for viewing. Better yet, hundreds of titles can be stored within your new library—on a single microchip. There are a variety of e-readers from different manufacturers. You can also read e-books on your PC or laptop computer. (Please note that Ellora's Cave does not endorse any specific brands.

You can check our websites at www.ellorascave.com or www.cerridwenpress.com for information we make available to new consumers.)

3. ***Mobility***. Because your new e-library consists of only a microchip within a small, easily transportable e-reader, your entire cache of books can be taken with you wherever you go.
4. ***Personal Viewing Preferences.*** Are the words you are currently reading too small? Too large? Too... ANNOYING? Paperback books cannot be modified according to personal preferences, but e-books can.
5. ***Instant Gratification.*** Is it the middle of the night and all the bookstores near you are closed? Are you tired of waiting days, sometimes weeks, for bookstores to ship the novels you bought? Ellora's Cave Publishing sells instantaneous downloads twenty-four hours a day, seven days a week, every day of the year. Our webstore is never closed. Our e-book delivery system is 100% automated, meaning your order is filled as soon as you pay for it.

Those are a few of the top reasons why electronic books are replacing paperbacks for many avid readers.

As always, Ellora's Cave and Cerridwen Press welcome your questions and comments. We invite you to email us at Comments@ellorascave.com or write to us directly at Ellora's Cave Publishing Inc., 1056 Home Avenue, Akron, OH 44310-3502.

Cerridwen, the Celtic Goddess of wisdom, was the muse who brought inspiration to storytellers and those in the creative arts. Cerridwen Press encompasses the best and most innovative stories in all genres of today's fiction. Visit our site and discover the newest titles by talented authors who still get inspired - much like the ancient storytellers did, once upon a time.

Cerridwen Press

www.cerridwenpress.com

Discover for yourself why readers can't get enough of the multiple award-winning publisher Ellora's Cave.

Whether you prefer e-books or paperbacks, be sure to visit EC on the web at www.ellorascave.com for an erotic reading experience that will leave you breathless.